Mandey Nicholas   Jun 1992

GW00502641

THE
CALLING

THE
CALLING

RICHARD SANFORD

NEW ENGLISH LIBRARY

British Library Cataloguing in Publication Data
Sanford, Richard
  The calling.
  I. Title
  823'.914 [F]

ISBN 0-450-51072-7

Copyright © 1990 by Richard Sanford

First published in Great Britain 1990

All rights reserved. No part of this publication may be
reproduced or transmitted in any form or by any means,
electronic or mechanical, including photocopying,
recording, or any information storage and retrieval system,
without either prior permission in writing from the
publisher or a licence permitting restricted copying.
In the United Kingdom such licences are issued by the
Copyright Licensing Agency, 33–34 Alfred Place, London WC1E 7DP.

Published by New English Library,
a hardcover imprint of Hodder and Stoughton,
a division of Hodder and Stoughton Ltd,
Mill Road, Dunton Green, Sevenoaks, Kent TN13 2YA
Editorial Office: 47 Bedford Square, London WC1B 3DP

Typeset by Hewer Text Composition Services, Edinburgh
Printed in Great Britain by St Edmundsbury Press Ltd, Bury St Edmunds, Suffolk
and bound by BPCC Hazell Books Ltd, Aylesbury, Bucks.

Darkness has called to darkness . . .

As a Plane Tree by the Water, Robert Lowell

Part 1
Alpenhurst

1

Rising in the air, pausing, then dropping like an icicle from a ledge, the spike sank in deep. Surprisingly deep.

A quick yank couldn't free it. Only by working it forwards and backwards, side to side. Pushing against the hole it had made, pulling it wider. Then lifting.

In the shadow of the roof, the evening air was cool. The scent of pine and balsam fir carried from the heavy trees across the wide lawn. From far off, the smell of the lake was pure, clear, like a vesper bell.

Surprisingly deep.

Not that anyone was left to surprise. The grounds were quiet. The caretaker had gone.

The old house stood mutely behind, and the only sound under the overhang of the roof at the corner was like a rough whisper. It could have been a hoarse breath at the end of a phone in the senseless pit of night. Or a sardonic whistle through dry lips. Or a July evening settling through sun-dried grass at the edge of the woods.

No one else heard it, the sound like air slipping up through a dry throat, and there was no one to see. Nothing could have seen but the red tailed hawk.

Two thousand feet up, circling on its wide bank of air, the sound in its ears was a thin rush. Far below, the oblong lake flashed white, like a chunk of mirror, in the corner of its eye.

It could have spotted what was happening beside the great house, beyond the black fingers that stretched across the grass from the tall firs. The hawk's eyes, like precision lenses, could have tightened on the spike as it rose just inside the square shade of the eave then drilled down in the same patch of shadow at the corner of the long slate-coloured roof.

It was drawn to imperfection. Any quick glint of a blade would catch its eye, or the slash of something not quite a blade but a blade of sorts, a kind of claw.

It would spot the small detail, even in the forest, the hard, sharp whistle that ripped the leaves, long before the dark burst and the gushing warmth it could nearly taste on its black whip tongue, or the dead weight going down on heavy knees then tilting, pitching forwards, mouth gaping in wet rot.

The spike rose again and hovered there as though considering its target. The air was still.

Down. Tock.

Down and in deep. Tock. A hollow pop like suction in an empty skull.

There. That would do.

Dark patches spread over the grass. Long before they joined the shadow of the eave, the spike had been ground back and forth and lifted free.

Hands had reinserted it into the hole it had come from, out in the middle of the caretaker's green lawn. The hose, reattached, lay in precisely the same path, the wavy green tracing from the old house to the sprinkler. No one had seen.

In the patch of shade made by the corner overhang, the cross-shaped holes in the black dirt had been tamped shut. Hands had patted and smoothed the deep punctures made with the spike. The hands had closed all but one – so whoever saw it would know.

As deepening shadows spread all the way to the eave, the heady smell of firs and matted needles and rich, dry earth in evening slipped from the mouth of the forest. It settled like a dark breath against the walls of the old house which sat cooling and waiting.

2

Dana touched her lip with her tongue and looked down. The road was winding up a steeper gradient. Faces of sheared-off granite walled the left side of the incline, and black tree roots stuck straight out of the cliffside like bony fingers. Below the roots, small slides had piled stones by the pavement in natural cairns.

The lake lay somewhere on the right side of the car, but they were too far away to see it. When Dana looked down the hill, it was like a wonderland forest. White firs and balsam firs beside the road towered above them like sleepy giants. She could see the same kinds of trees from the middles and tops as they descended the hill. It was mysterious and thrilling looking down on the tall ones from above.

"Louis, you have to see this!" She pulled her knees up under her, rising in the seat, and gave his leg a squeeze.

"Okay, okay. You're supposed to be telling me where I'm going. They don't mark the damn roads up here. They just assume you know . . . Wow, that is nice." He glanced over the side for a moment.

"Nice," Dana said, grinning at him behind her shades.

Was this really happening to them? She shook her head. She slipped her fingers into her black hair and shook it out. Nice, all right. Then she slid back down in the seat and traced their progress on the Altos Realty map.

She knew Louis was in no mood to miss the turn. They had already coasted past the cut-off to Tallac Lane, the unlikely-looking two-lane access road, and had spent half an hour getting back. She studied the map. In the next ten minutes they saw no other cars on the winding road, but Dana knew it was coming, just beyond the Lapis Creek bridge.

"There!" A mailbox on a bright yellow post was coming into view on the left. The brochure had mentioned it at the end of the property.

"There's no name," Louis protested as they got close.

"Turn here, just turn."

He did, and it was suddenly darker. The little road entered a heavy patch of trees that clumped together, making a dense canopy above the car. They bounded down the narrow dirt trail. Ten yards in front of them, the road made a turn and disappeared in the trees.

"You sure?" He glanced at her before they took the bend to no return.

Dana flashed on the possibility that they were trespassing, soon to be spotted by the owner or his henchmen, jumped by some crazy pack of backwoods inbred types. She took comfort in the fact that what you could imagine rarely happened.

"Yes!" she shouted.

They rolled around the bend and the car began to vibrate, but it was a pleasant vibration, the kind that comes with a transition to stone surface after rutted dirt road. A little farther along, past the granite cinders and wider flat stones, the trees opened and a token of civilisation appeared like a mirage, not quite real, a patch of grass under bright sun.

The sky opened and the grass was all around them. The stone road had become a driveway, rising gently up a long sloping yard.

"See! I knew it!"

"You knew it all right."

It looked bigger than their memories of the slides. It was only two storeys, but the high roof gave Alpenhurst dominance over the two-hundred-foot yard. Tall firs framed the back and grew close enough to cast shade on the west wing.

The driveway ran along the east side of the yard and circled back on itself. A second branch of the drive looped past the tall front door. The short east wing was a single storey that joined under the broad overhang of the main roof.

12

The bay windows on both floors would look dazzling in the morning light in midsummer, but afternoon shadows had subdued them. The same shadows fell over the windshield as Louis and Dana pulled up before the front door, peaks of shade from the broad roof that overspread Alpenhurst like dark wings.

"Hey, where are you going?"

Dana was out the door, running into the yard. She turned and looked back. Her face was pure delight.

"It's magnificent, Louis."

He got out too and looked up, suitably awestruck.

"Of course it's magnificent. What did you expect? Let's rent out that entire wing. We'd never know they were there."

Dana surveyed the house, especially the bay windows. She thought back to the slides they saw during the presentation by Altos. The breakfast nook was on the west end. She spotted the rose garden outside it on the left side of the house, somewhat smaller than the pictures had made it seem, but a garden nonetheless.

She took a deep breath. She couldn't quibble about the rose garden. *One of the select timeshare properties in the world*, the Altos representative had said at the raffle, and Dana recalled it as her eyes roamed over the spreading chalet, a Black Forest manor with walls dripping in ivy and a huge door beneath an arched lintel.

The four bedrooms were all upstairs. The set of windows on the left were the guest bedrooms, and the bay window on the right . . . Dana blinked. She squinted at the bay window of the master bedroom and blinked again.

She thought for a moment that something had moved there, just inside, behind the curtain on the right. But now the white panel was hanging undisturbed. A bird had flown by, reflecting for an instant in the glass, or it had been her imagination.

"Shall we?" Daintily between forefinger and thumb, Louis was holding up the keys.

Dana glanced at the window again, just for a moment, then joined him. They each took a suitcase and climbed

13

the broad front steps of cement and stone. There was a heavy metallic click as he turned the key in the tall front door that was dark as railroad ties.

At the same moment, in the back of the house, a door was easing shut. The lock quietly turning.

3

They went in and put the bags down, and for a long moment they could only stare. On the right the living-room ceiling soared upwards in dark beams. Straight ahead, a staircase rose towards the back wall then turned and ascended. A leaded window admitted enough light to reveal intricate carving on the dark panels that framed the stairs.

In the room a long brown sofa, comfortably sagged, sat across from two stuffed chairs, an Ansel Adams photo book on the heavy coffee table between them.

"Is it for us?" An elaborate fruit basket occupied the rest of the table, and Dana crossed into the living room and plucked an envelope from it. "It's from Altos." She passed the card to Louis, a welcome to Alpenhurst with the company logo – isosceles mountains – in the background.

"I know what's in here – it has to be." Dana strode the other way, past the stairs, and reached for the double doors to the west wing. "This is going to be my favourite room, I know it." She turned the knobs.

She stepped into the breakfast nook, an airy, intimate room. On the far side of white table and chairs, French windows opened on the little plot of roses.

"I know what I'm looking for," Louis called, and she followed him into the next room. The kitchen looked old and tall and practical with cabinets above and below, long white tile counters flanking the sink, and heavy pots and pans suspended above the gas range.

"All right!" He was through the kitchen, holding open a redwood door. By the time she reached him, he was already setting the thermostat. "This is going to be stop number

14

one on the path to ultimate decadence. Nice to be home, isn't it?"

They stood together in the door of the sauna. In a minute, a little heat began to rise from the stones in the corner. Dana was thinking they could have won the pocket calculator in the raffle, or one of the colour TVs. Instead they had the Alpenhurst sauna all to themselves for a month – and the rest of the house.

"Let's build up some heat," he said, closing the door, backing out.

"In the meantime, care for a snack? Wait'll you see what I saw."

"Nachos? Escargot?"

He followed her back through the kitchen. They entered the dining room and Dana spread her arms. "Ta da."

Above a wide table surrounded by eight chairs hung an elaborate chandelier. French provincial china filled a tall cherry hutch, and windows with quaint interior shutters looked on to the back yard and the forest.

"Wasn't this one of the slides?" She was thinking of the presentation at the contest. Louis joined her at the wall opposite the hutch.

"I think you're right." It was one of a series of old photos of Alpenhurst. They were all mounted in dark frames, and beneath each picture was a legend of a paragraph or two.

The first shot showed the house as it once had been, somewhat smaller but seeming just as grand, ladies under parasols and bonnets and whiskered gentlemen in light suits standing stiffly, one foot forwards on the lawn. She read the note.

"Alpenhurst was constructed in 1897, the second home of San Francisco mining magnate R.S. Marquand. On summer evenings at the turn of the century, the Marquands received guests from the city who typically arrived at Agate Bay then travelled the rest of the way in carriages sent down to meet them."

They moved to the next picture, a similar view, but the trees were blackened and part of the east wing was charred. Louis read the legend.

15

"In August 1919 a portion of the grounds of Alpenhurst was destroyed by fire. A bucket brigade from the town of Lapis – and an opportune shift in the wind – finally spared the house."

"And they restored it." Dana went on to the next photo.

"The Hale family completely restored the east wing and added the porte-cochère, which afforded shelter for guests who arrived during inclement weather. The Hales installed leaded glass in the entrance and in windows on both floors. In addition, the original first floor was replaced with tessellated flooring throughout, a mosaic of beech and oak laid by craftsmen from Washington State."

"Jacks Peak, Echo Summit, Boomerang Lake, Blood-sucker Lake. Check this one – Lover's Leap." Louis was surveying a wall map of the Tahoe area. In the centre lay Lake Tahoe, the twenty-mile-long jewel of the Sierras on the border of California and Nevada. The miles of beaches, the glittering casinos on the lake's south end and, a little farther out, the fabulously beautiful ski slopes made Tahoe a paradisal playground in winter and summer, day and night. Other smaller lakes and peaks on the map dotted the wilder-looking expanse around the big lake. Louis chuckled at Lover's Leap, but at the same time he imagined how terrifying it could be to be lost out there. In the winter you could make an SOS with rocks or branches in the snow. Funny, in the summer . . . it could be harder.

Tessellated, he thought suddenly, and checked the floor. The geometry of alternating woods was like parquet but more intricate. A puzzle under foot, a grand design.

Dana glanced out of the dining room towards the foot of the stairs. She didn't like them. They were making her feel cold, and at first she didn't know why. Then it got clearer.

It had been her imagination. Definitely. She had made it up – the one behind the curtain in the room up there. If so, she could fix it, that was for sure. She knew what she could do. When she was finished, there would only be . . . PULL OUT! Get conscious.

16

And she did. She didn't sink in that time, only skimmed the surface. But she was being drawn away. She began walking towards the stairs. Louis was saying something.

The view out of the front window caught her eye. Whoever it was could have come across that lawn. There could be others. They despised her sudden good luck, her decadent little sojourn. Ragged creatures from the city were dragging up the long yard, ones Dana might have seen that morning, heaped in a doorway that smelled of urine, wrapped in filthy blankets, bare soles clubbed by night sticks, pitched out of paddy wagons into cells and morgues and puddles of vomit and two-dollar red wine. They wanted a little of their own back, that was all. They were staggering in close, paying Dana a visit, half a dozen of them, sores on their faces. The one in front with the torn coat, shoulders steaming, was lifting his hand –

"Don't you think so?" Louis was walking past her.

"Think so what?" she said, shaking her head. Not normal.

"I said, this must be a den. Don't you think?"

He was already opening the door on the other side of the stairs. Her heart was racing. What else was new? She could tell it was, but barely. It was so common it was second nature, just the other way of being. Downshift. Slow it down. Not normal, thoughts like that weren't. Neither was she, and Dana could not recall a time when she hadn't known that deep down. It didn't keep her from feeling cold. Lost. She glanced again at the front window and, beyond, the empty front yard.

Louis stepped into the sitting room. Tall bookcases filled with hardbound volumes covered an entire wall, and he noticed a set, something like Trollope or Balzac or, he hoped, Conan Doyle. A brandy decanter and glasses sat on a table between deep chairs. Behind him, he heard her bounding up, feet hitting the landing.

He left the room and followed, taking the stairs two at a time. At the top, the second-floor hall ran right and left. Louis turned right.

The first door opened on a bedroom with a graceful old

17

armoire and canopy bed. No Dana. Two other bedrooms lay at the end of the wing, a matching pair of guest rooms that shared a chimney stack, the fireplaces in the rooms built back-to-back. No Dana.

"Louis?" She sounded a little petulant or a little scared. It came from the far end of the hall.

There was only one door at the east end and it was open. That wing was darker, opposite the afternoon light that had begun to lose itself in the trees. As Louis headed towards the door, he noticed a window inside with white curtains and a reddish oriental rug that looked elegant, even in the shadows. What was that on the rug? A stain of some kind?

"Where were you?" Dana was standing at the other bay window, the one on the right that overlooked the yard.

"Exploring. I didn't know where you were." On the rug, a shadow from the dresser and the lamp. A Rorschach of a shadow, that was all.

"Louis, is this real? Are we really here?" She shook him by the arms then pirouetted and flopped back on the bed. It was a four-poster, too luxuriously large to be very old. The posts rose five feet above the king-sized comforter. Louis cruised over, arms out straight like a plane, and flopped down too.

"I feel like a lottery winner," he said, "a dumb-chance millionaire. Freak of nature."

"No way. These things don't just happen, you know that." She kicked her shoes off over the side and pulled her feet up on the bed. He liked the way her breasts flattened out to the sides under the Danskin top, nipples visible under black. "There's a very good reason for everything."

"We must have paid our dues or something." He started rubbing her chest.

"We have to make a fire tonight," she announced, sitting up, staring at the fireplace in the corner opposite the bed. Why did she do that? Was she pulling away?

"It's the middle of summer," he said.

"Of course!"

It was a great-looking fireplace, directly above the one

18

in the living room. She lay back down and snuggled up, and he felt better. Of course it was the middle of summer. They were really there. What that meant was starting to sink in. It meant that it didn't matter whether it was the middle of summer. If you felt like making a fire, you made it without thinking about why not. It meant loosen up.

And it didn't matter so much that Louis had a total of seven working days – a week and a half including the weekend – to participate with his wife in paradise, whereas she had almost three weeks off. He had arranged another week, on the condition that he would call in every day to see if they needed him in the office.

He tried to remind himself that feeling bad about it was silly. It had nothing to do with real value, maturity, wisdom or worth to the world. It did reflect simple seniority in the organisation. That could be construed, if one were in the mood to be tough on oneself, as a function of the amount of time she, in this case, had been on track with her career and he hadn't. In other words, he would have been able to pull three weeks of vacation the way Dana had if he had been at Sutton for three years instead of a little over eleven months. As it was, it was one week and on-call.

"A fire it will be," he declared. "But first, what do you say we check out the sauna?"

"Okay, let's get the suitcases."

"What for?"

"I want some stuff – moisturiser. It's good for you. You should use it too."

"Sure. You stay. Last in, first out," he volunteered, pushing out of bed, feeling the drive in the small of his back. He really just wanted to jog his thoughts. By the time he hauled the bags up, he almost had it. He went into the washroom and ran the water cold, splashed his face, and concentrated on clearing the brain of thoughts of vacation time.

He was pulling his shirt off as he went back into the bedroom. Dana had been unpacking, and clothes lay in piles of colour on the bed.

"Louis," she turned to face him. "Do you think I should wear this?"

As usual, he liked the way she looked, the smile that seemed to take over her face and eyes, the little catlike upturned corners of her mouth, and the body that looked ready enough for some gymnastics. She was always in shape, too thin if anything. And she knew what he thought about the silky camisole.

She had a familiar, mischievous look. She flipped the black fandango over his head and slinked it slowly down the side of his face. Then she was rubbing his chest with it. He reached for her hip.

She was too quick, and she had surprise on her side. She tackled him and they both went over into the clothes.

They were laughing and tickling each other, then she rolled free and knelt in the middle of the bed. She began to peel up the bottom of her pullover, and he remembered she was braless. The shirt popped over her head.

She shook out her hair and watched him slyly. Dana wasn't heavy on top, but her breasts were firm and high. His tongue remembered the taste as it came closer. Sometimes she wore a little perfume there, and he nestled in, skin like warm silk against his face.

China Rain, that was the scent today. Her nipple was hardening under his tongue. Why did she wear perfume between her breasts some days and not others? Did she know what would happen? Did she make it happen as surely as her hand slipping between his legs would make him leave it all behind, the on-call days and the adolescent real world?

He grabbed the backs of her thighs and pulled, and Dana dropped backwards on to the pillows. He knew she liked it. He popped the button on her jeans and she unzipped, and he started to strip too. They didn't undress each other any more, as they often did in the early days. It wasn't really a loss of romance, Louis thought, it was a gain in speed, and there was much to be said for speed sometimes.

This was one of those times. They were ready quickly, more than ready. He kissed her and their mouths opened into each other. She bit his cheek a little and then hard enough that reflex pulled him away.

20

She lay back on the pillow, lips parted and a little puffed, like models' lips when they pose.

He slipped in and a low groan rose in her throat. Then she was kneading his shoulders and chest and grinding against him and pulling back.

Louis was not thinking about careers and vacations. It was like blues, he was thinking, and he was the bluesman. All those old black men with no money, ripped off by agents and producers and rock bands of white boys – all they had were their songs and their cocks. Louis was the bluesman. He only appeared middle-class to the rest of the world. He was the bluesman within. No debonair bullshit. Right, baby, right?

In the next moment Dana was off the pillows, pushing her head and shoulders into him like a wrestler bridging out of a pin. She didn't have the weight to push him over, but he rolled sideways until she was on top.

She was in her element then; there was no denying it. He had no complaints. It wasn't bad to lie back and let her do the work, but soon he was working hard just to hold back, make it last. Dana didn't make it easy.

There was no way to take his eyes off her. It was the way she was a lot of the time, he felt, only more so. She had a supremely attractive quality of always seeming a little out of control. Making love with Dana only turned her volume up. It was strangely beautiful watching her, but a little unnerving. It seemed to him that it wasn't passion exactly, but it was hard to say just how it was different, especially at that moment with their heat and their smells mixing like combustible charges.

Then Dana's head was shaking back and forth and back and forth. It seemed that she was transported, gone out of herself somewhere, and Louis was hanging on to her body which ground and rocked on him. Then their hips were firing into each other until he was gone too, blurred out of himself along the trajectory Dana took, but somewhere to the side, or not so far.

She collapsed on him and they lay together. Floating, she called it, the recovery phase. To Louis it felt more

21

like surfacing, rising into calm water, serene blue above him when he opened his eyes. But he could picture Dana floating through the air, definitely. She'd be re-entering, parachuting down through the blue from whatever planet she had visited. " 'Scuse me while I kiss the sky."

They kissed lazily a few times. Eventually he rolled out on to his feet and started to head for the bathroom, stopping to switch on the TV with the remote control beside the bed.

"The Berkeley seismology lab reports it was centred near Livermore and tipped the scales at 4.8 on the Richter." The shaker had hit after they left the city. They hadn't felt a thing on the road. "That was no lightweight, folks."

"You're telling me," Louis told the TV, thinking only partly of the quake.

"Did you hear that?" Dana shouted from the bed. "Almost five!" When he didn't answer for a moment, she called out again.

"Yeah, almost five," he said, concentration elsewhere. No blood, but not far from it either. He was inches from the bathroom mirror, studying his cheek and the mildly disturbing pink bite the size of a human front tooth.

Louis ladled water on and a steam cloud rose. Dana was standing wrapped in a green plush bath towel from breast to thigh.

"This should be just right in a minute."

He spooned on one more ladle and pulled the door shut tight. The aroma of redwood was like pure incense.

She climbed up on the seat and cleared the small porthole window with her hand. He joined her and they put their heads together and looked out.

"It's so beautiful here," she said softly, one hand on his leg. The window faced the back yard and the forest. The tall firs looked deep green, nearly black, in the late afternoon light, and they threw long shadows on the lawn.

"I think this is going to be all right," he said, massaging her back. It was moist between the shoulder blades.

She got down and stood in front of him.

"I think it's going to be perfectly wonderful," she said.

22

"It's like a special chance. We can catch up on each other."
She undid the towel and stood there, quietly naked before
him.

He got down and dropped his towel and they stood
front-to-front. The steam had made a delicate film on her
skin, and the soft light in the sauna gave it a tantalising
glow. They were deliciously close, just barely touching.
She smiled softly and stood on her toes to kiss him.

Dana put herself into the kiss, concentrated on it. That
was unusual, she realised. Usually, when they kissed, she
was thinking about something else. She didn't like it, but
that's what time did. It was pretty natural, wasn't it?
But now it could be different. She could take the time
to concentrate, to feel his tongue with her tongue, the
not-quite-prickly texture of his beard on her upper lip and
chin. She wanted the kisses to last now, and be tender, to
show him that she still had that side, that she wasn't all
consumed by career, frustrated and bitchy and businesslike
as it seemed so often she had to be.

She wanted those kisses to be magical. It seemed that
they could be. If kisses could ever make time stand still,
this was the time and the place. They were stroking each
other, and she loved the way it was going to last – it was
like floating.

If the kisses could stop time, why couldn't they rewind
it? She was thinking about their garden apartment in the
Mission and sleeping late before they got their first jobs
in the city. Guerrero Street flooded back: kids shouting
in the street at dinner time, ghetto blasters heading for
Dolores Park, the back door they left open in the spring
with the view through the screen of the back stairs and
porches painted grey with bright clothes drying on lines.

She had the job at the paper then, the *Business Journal*.
How many years ago? Three? No, she had been at Micro
T three years. Guerrero Street would be four years ago in
November.

Where had a year gone? They had asked questions like
that numerous times before. There really wasn't much to say
about it at ages thirty-six and -seven, not remembering

the exact point when the years had started to gallop and blur.

They were living too fast, she knew. There wasn't even time to remember you were living. Except now. They were being given a chance. Things didn't happen by accident. They could wind it back a moment at a time. A kiss at a time.

Louis and Dana concentrated on their private place, delighting in each other, taking their rare chance to let the world go by. It was less than a possibility, the farthest thought from their minds, that across the yard, beyond the shadows and beneath the ancient tall trees which cast them, eyes were watching a round window, looking in hotly through the hole in the steam.

4

Brian Thomas popped the second grape into his mouth and kept driving. It was as sweet as the first. They wouldn't be missed. It wasn't as though he had pulled them from the front or the top where it would have been noticeable. They were just sitting there, like tiny Easter eggs in the green packing at the bottom of the fruit basket. He had placed it on the table, rotated it just a bit, nestled the small envelope between the kiwi and the peach. When he left the basket had been in perfect order – also the house.

He had nothing to be ashamed of. He had done his part. Everything was on target. That wasn't the reason he had waited to make the call. It had been too close for comfort. He had wanted more distance on the downhill road, out of the tangle of the hills and away from the chilly darkness that always seemed to come on too early, cast by the tall trees.

The steeper hills he had left behind. The road had unwound and was starting to flatten. Brian could feel a spot tightening in his gut. He considered carefully what he was about to say and hear. He lifted the receiver and slowed. He was reluctant to hear the voice again. He had every reason to be. He punched the numbers in rapid succession and put the receiver to his ear.

It rang twice before there was an answer.

"Hello, it's Brian. They've arrived."

Quiet. It was more than a pause, he thought, but he couldn't tell what it was exactly. Laughter?

"Yes." The old man's voice sounded like a door on bad hinges.

Of course, Brian realised. He knew.

"Your diligence has rewarded you," the voice went on, "also your faith. And now, as you know, we have our bargain."

The words dropped like weights. If Brian had wanted to back out, he had passed the point.

"Yes," he forced himself to say, "can you tell me when – "

"When the time comes, you will know."

"Yes, but if you could give me some idea, I could prepare more fully. I want to do what's asked of me and . . ." Even as he had started to speak, he suspected that no one was listening. When he was sure, he stopped. He listened for a while to the empty line. The road was slipping beneath him.

Brian was winded. He was envisioning the old man again, recalling the exact room and all the eyes on him, like animal eyes, rodent eyes, the old man's eyes. For some reason he was thinking of the hands, the long fingers and heavy knuckles, and the sallow colour of his nails.

In their sauna towels, Louis and Dana sat on the old couch in the living room. It wasn't nine yet, but the ride and the steam and their duet upstairs were catching up with them. She had the coffee-table book of stunning Yosemite photos on her lap and was turning pages, but neither of them could keep their eyes open.

"Enough thrills for one day?" He was grinning at her lazily, saturated with bliss.

"If you insist."

She heaved Ansel Adams back on to the table, and they both struggled up. The remains of pastrami sandwiches from the Genoa Deli in North Beach sat on the table too. She reached for their plates.

"Halt. No work. You're forbidden until tomorrow." He took Dana by the shoulders and began guiding her towards the stairs. "Maybe not tomorrow. Maybe we'll just let the crud pile up. The password is *mañana*." They started up but he felt her resisting.

"Something wrong?"

"No."

"Sure?" he pressed, sounding nervous. She knew what he was thinking.

"No, really. I'm fine." He hoped it was true and she knew it. It was no time for an episode – they both wanted to believe that. "I was just wondering, that's all. About Rhonda and Brian. I think I should call."

"I bet it could wait until morning." He had a condescending look. They had been over this ground before.

Since they had won, Dana hadn't felt right about Rhonda and Brian. They were the only reason she and Louis had been at the contest at all. Of course, it was true that the invitations would have gone to waste otherwise. It was Rhonda's parents' thirty-fifth anniversary, and Brian had got tickets for Merce Cunningham a month earlier. That was why they had offered Dana and Louis their invitations. They couldn't have gone anyway.

Nevertheless, Dana had been worried. Were they really jealous? Would there be hard feelings? It had troubled her until she had asked Rhonda directly. Dana had felt guilty. Not Louis, so much. He was happy, he was grateful, he had told them so. He had it in perspective.

Guilt. Call it by its name, she thought, the old nemesis. She knew where that one came from well enough. She could see the form it took, but not clearly, not quite. It was like a caricature in her memory, a cartoon. Mama. She was too far away for Dana to see her clearly or too far inside.

She could almost see her, but she was like a statue in

her mind's eye, not quite alive, not fully formed. Dana saw steely hair and the lines of struggle in her face. What were those on her hands? Stigmata? Did the statue's red eyes roll up like Mary's in mourning? STOP IT! She would stop it. Mother of God have mercy.

Dana and guilt, they were no strangers. Was it gnawing at her because she was thinking of the phone? Her mother had asked for their number in Tahoe and Dana had promised it, but now she wasn't sure, not sure at all.

She couldn't do much about her mother. She could do something about Rhonda and Brian. It would be a nice gesture to call. Keep it on that level – adult all the way. Her therapist would approve.

"I'll just be a minute." She grinned and popped back down into the living room.

What difference, Louis thought, and started back up the stairs.

"What?" she said before he reached the landing. He turned.

"I didn't say anything."

She was going to ask what he meant by making that sound but stopped. Instead she smiled and nodded and picked up the phone. He hadn't cleared his throat or sighed impatience. It had been something else she had heard. It was like a quick breath – dry, reedy-sounding.

Louis didn't smile back, just checked her for a moment, then kept going up.

Dana put the phone to her ear and listened to the steady dialling tone.

He decided to brush his teeth and forget it. He turned the old brass faucet and the water gushed country-cold. She would do what she wanted, he knew. Not wanted exactly, but needed – that was more like it. No need to make a case out of it.

He wondered for a moment if they should invite Brian and Rhonda. They had extended the offer before, just after they had won the contest. They had laughed it off at the time.

27

It didn't seem practical. Still, they might be persuaded. In Alpenhurst, they weren't exactly cramped.

Even as he thought it, it felt dutiful and not very appealing. He liked them well enough, but they weren't really that close. There were basic differences that made Louis feel something like underpaid when they were all together. Although they had other friends who were good at making money, it seemed tangential to who they really were. Brian and Rhonda never talked about money, but it was always around somehow. It seemed to Louis that they were all running a race of some kind, out of breath but still going on vicious cunning and unquenchable desire, although they appeared to be sitting calmly in living rooms or behaving cordially at parties, artificially animated or casually still.

There was something else. He didn't like the way Brian looked at Dana sometimes. He was attracted to her, Louis knew, which was all right in itself, but occasionally he didn't turn off the look at the right time, and that was offensive. If he had to admit it to himself, that was probably the real reason he wasn't crazy about Brian and Rhonda staying. A day or two might be acceptable; any more would be tense.

Better to leave this one alone. Saturday night, he thought. They might be out anyway. A movie? Dancing at the Fairmont? A poor substitute for paradise. Louis grinned in the mirror, toothpaste in his teeth.

Dana stood at the corner of the sofa and counted the rings. She hoped Rhonda would answer. It wasn't that she disliked Brian. She was just more comfortable talking to a woman. That was natural. Or was it? Two. She could talk as easily with Louis's friend Tom as she could with his girlfriend Gina. Usually, after the ice was broken, it might even be easier to talk with men. Three.

It wasn't that way with Brian and Rhonda. She remembered the last time they were over for dinner. It was the night they passed along the invitation. Brian seemed more than casually interested in her. Dana had felt it before. He had ways of looking, and there were a lot of stolen glances

28

which he thought she didn't see. She flashed on leaving the living room for the after-dinner coffee, catching his reflection in the glass door of the hutch, his eyes on her. Four. He answered, on tape.

"Hello. You've reached the mechanical marvel of Brian and Rhonda Thomas. We can't come to the phone . . ."

Dana relaxed. She sat down on the back of the sofa and waited for the beep.

The message she left was simple. It was incredible there, like paradise. Didn't they want to come, if just for a weekend? When she hung up, she felt better.

"That was quick," he said.

"They're out. Night owls."

Good, he thought, but didn't say it. It wasn't hard to imagine keeping the place to themselves. Whatever happened, he would take it as it came.

Flat on his back on the four-poster, Louis surveyed the bedroom. Everything was tranquillising – the beamed ceiling, the dark bureaux and chiffonier, the fireplace they hadn't fired up yet but would. There was *mañana*. The sound of water running in the bathroom almost lulled him to sleep.

He was half-thinking that some kind of simple country life should be possible. But how to swing it? What would he have to do to stay there for ever? That was the question. Work in construction? Train to be a forest ranger? If he wasn't too old. A chilling thought. And where would they wind up? Not exactly in Alpenhurst. More likely in an A-frame cabin on a fair-weather road.

It didn't matter. They were there tonight. They would sleep a primitive sleep in the bosom of the woods.

In a few minutes Dana slipped in beside him and snuggled up. Consciousness was dimming, closing down. It felt as though she had lifted up a corner of his dream and slipped in. She said something and he answered, but a moment later he couldn't remember. He was driving up a mountain road, trees standing like tall witnesses on either side.

29

They were in a strange bed in the old rambling house that had begun creaking oddly, settling in the night. Nevertheless, five minutes after Dana joined him in the four-poster, they were both asleep.

In the city, in an apartment on Gough Street, Brian Thomas checked the pulse on his answering machine. He slid the volume bar forward, but not too far, rewound, and shifted to play. Behind him in the dark room, a lamp with a long silver neck bowed over the arm of a black leatherette sofa. The smoky plastic doors of a stereo system reflected the thinnest of light, like lake water on a moonless night, and a glass coffee table held that film of light also, in a low rectangle before the sofa.

As he listened to her voice, he stared out of the broad picture window, down the hill at the Saturday night river of lights on Lombard Street and at the white buildings of the Marina district a few blocks beyond. He heard what Dana was saying and more. He smiled to himself as he listened to the cadence of her phrases that started out evenly then rushed to the next idea. That was her way, as he knew well. There was also that tone that seemed to suit her especially, a slight lilt like a plucked string. The message ended and he shifted the bar back to record.

When the green light came on, he stood and only watched it for a moment. The shower had helped after the long drive, but the sound of the other voice, dry as kindling, was still with him. The words kept re-forming in his head, echoing in the old man's tone, chafing inside, along the nerve. He was counting on the Cabernet. It was a full-bottle night.

He looked far down the hill, over the Marina and the bay, where Angel Island would be visible in the daylight. He tried to centre his thoughts there, in the hills populated with deer, surrounded by water. He tried to focus on the island, but soon he was seeing curly black hair, watching his own reflection in the glass. He turned and left the living room.

In the bedroom Rhonda was standing at her dresser, back turned. The sleeveless nightgown hung straight from her shoulders to the floor. She was undoing an earring.

30

"That was Dana. She called to say they got there and it's great. That's nice, isn't it?"

Rhonda put the earring into a box and began to remove the other. Brian turned to his dresser and slipped off his watch and laid it face-up. She began to hum a tune softly, something like a lullaby. "Hush little baby, don't you cry." Brian guessed the tune. Da da da da da lullaby. He heard the other earring plop in among her jewellery, and the lid closed tight.

5

First there was the perfume. Whether it was really a scent, like the smell of the lake or the fragrance of pine and balsam, or whether it was a thing of its own, more material than essence, was hard to say. Either way, it was musky and effective, even at a distance, on the other side of thick manzanita.

She took an animal stance in the clearing, feet shoulder-width apart, head high, back slightly arched. She was running fingers through dark hair.

Even from that distance, behind dense cover at the edge, it was possible to sense the firm swell of her hip and thigh against the yellow cotton dress that clung like a long camisole. Her raised arms lifted her breasts. A cooling breeze could harden the nipples, make the dark points visible.

Rose-coloured evening light slanted into the clearing, just catching the nest of delicate hairs in her underarms. It looked soft to the touch, like cat's fur.

She squatted down and fingered a wildflower. Mountain phlox and goldenrod shimmered around her. The yellow curve of her buttocks and thigh would have felt firm and full to a man's palm, or to a predator that kept a watch for solid flesh.

She picked several flowers, enough for a small bouquet of purple and gold. When she stood up, she smelled them for

31

a moment then, choosing carefully, dropped all the flowers but one. She began to stroll casually through the clearing in the direction of the woods.

The one who watched her, magnetised by her slow walk and by her scent, was forced to wait, safely hidden until she had crossed to the far side of the clearing. She paused, languorously fixing the flower above her ear. Then she moved on.

Soon the girl in the yellow dress, a purple phlox in her hair, was choosing her steps in the woods, crossing the moist, dark layers of leaves between the patches of sun.

She seemed oblivious to the possibility that she had been followed, that someone or something could have made its way silently through the manzanita around the perimeter of the little clearing to the spot where she had entered the woods. Nothing in the way she moved suggested that she could feel hot eyes targeting her young back or hear the quick passes of a tongue across dry lips.

She stopped in an opening between trees. A strap of the yellow shift had fallen from her shoulder. She turned sideways from the waist and smoothed her palm slowly, admiringly, along her hip. She could have been a sculptor stroking marble. It seemed that she had found her private place.

But it was a painful place to the watcher forced to remain so far from her. He would have to be closer – close enough to cause her hair to flutter with a breath.

The bushes made a sound. She spun and stared and clutched both arms around her waist. She took one step backwards, then another, staring into the bushes, waiting for the rustling to happen again.

She turned and began to run into the trees, sidestepping clumps of juniper and old water-blackened ash in the ring of stones where a camper's fire had been. Steps followed her; heavy footsteps on the red and black leaves.

As she ran in farther, the woods grew dense. The footsteps crackling behind her covered savage, guttural breathing. She tore through a wall of bushes. A clearing, a fire oasis of charred stumps, opened suddenly beyond the shrubs.

32

Her pursuer reached the same bushes. He had closed the distance. She was a dozen feet away or less when his shoe caught a root and he pitched forwards on hands and knees.

His prey had stopped and turned and was staring down at him. All the fear had vanished, as though it had died. The roundish cat face had gone slack, drained of expression, flat and marginal-looking, like the face of an addict. The dark eyes with the tawdry mascara and wide brows still drew him in, but as he looked up, he saw a new strangeness there, a wildness beginning, something unnatural.

He knew he should be scrambling on hands and knees back into the woods. He had been seduced to the edge of savagery but it was over. Any man would have felt the same, coming on her like that in the warm clearing among the phlox and goldenrod.

He could move faster on his feet. He started to rise. His legs were shaking, muscles jerking like small traitors. His penis, which minutes before had strained against his pants, had shrivelled. The girl was nearly smiling. What am I doing here? he thought.

The girl took a step forwards. His pulse was racing. He crouched over his knees, rooted to the ground.

She was coming closer. What about her eyes? Was something burning in her head?

He was at work, jammed in the elevator, eyes front, trying to rise above the horrible miscalculation, the thing that was about to happen, that was happening. He could not move.

The elevator opened on the rim of a lake. He lay on the bed on the side of the back porch, safe and warm, and four years old. Beyond the tall windows, far past the dark yard and the breakwater, a string of lights, like tiny black beads, lay along the far shore of Lake St Clair.

The woman was a step away, her musk aroma flooding him. The strap had fallen down again, and her shoulder and arm looked sinewy and tense.

The lights across the lake were flickering. They were the last image on his brain as the woman's hand lashed out.

33

He heard it and felt only part of it. The fingers, cold and rigid as a steel claw, ripped at his throat. He stumbled and knelt down.

Her eyes were wide and shot with blood. A hissing came from between her teeth and white froth slipped over her lower lip.

He felt warm liquid on his chest. He tried to breathe and gagged. He coughed and gagged on his own blood.

A great ache exploded in his throat. He felt his bowels opening.

He swang at her but she clamped his arm and whipped the hand outward, wrenching the elbow. He toppled to the side, spitting blood, and she was on him.

She dropped a knee into the other shoulder, pinning him to the ground, then straddled him, hissing, foam dripping from her mouth and chin into his face.

Pausing, gathering strength, she felt impossibly heavy anchoring him from above, hair hanging down, blood eyes. Her lips curled back as she reached for his jaw. Fingers clamped behind the hinge of bone and dug in.

One superhuman pull ripped his jaw open like a gate. Blood fanned the air. In that instant, he didn't hear the crack like the sound of a chicken breastbone folded double. His own choking was louder, and the heaves of animal breath were over him and around him everywhere.

Louis didn't hear all of the sound, only the end, but he knew he had made it. Part gasp and part shout, it had been enough to wake Dana and he was hoping that it hadn't. He checked her. Her back was turned.

If the shout hadn't done it, she would probably sense him in another moment, propped halfway up on his elbow, heart charging, still breathing like a wild man or like a perfectly ordinary guy in the wrong place at the wrong time.

He lay down and let the heart run, as quietly as he could. Why in hell had he dreamed that? He couldn't remember the last time a dream had yanked him out of sleep.

He tried to piece it together, what it meant. Repressed anger? Repressed sexuality? He hadn't felt so repressed that

34

day – quite the opposite. In fact, he and Dana had been unusually licentious, sprung from their everyday lives.

That was it, he realised suddenly. It had been so good, he was feeling guilty somehow and had punished himself in the dream. That made sense, didn't it? Possibly. Whether or not it was the real reason was something else.

Dana rolled on to her back. He watched her shiny black hair, and her profile. He stopped worrying about her. She was doing better than he at the moment.

The backs of his arms and legs were wet and starting to get cold. He pulled up the blanket and forced his eyes closed. Maybe it was just the strange house or the new bed. That was more likely.

Louis's thoughts began to drift to the clearing and the girl again, but he pulled them away and tried counting his own breaths. Before lying still to wait for sleep, he knew he had to try one more thing, trusting that Dana wouldn't wake up and ask what he was doing, feeling first on one side and then the other the vulnerable spot at the base of the ear where the jaw's hinge met the throat.

6

She got up first in the morning, and by the time Louis made it to the kitchen, Dana was standing on a chair in her nightshirt, going through the last of the upper cabinets.

"So this is it, right?" He surveyed the box of Cap'n Crunch on the counter, half empty, donated by a previous occupant. How previous was the question. No problem. The label listed enough additives for generations. Whoever had cleaned had overlooked it.

"At least there's powdered milk," Dana said, descending with the box, making the best of it.

Louis pulled the refrigerator open.

"No," he said. "No." He held up a jar of Folger's crystals. "I can't do it. I have to have real coffee."

35

He didn't say why he had lost three hours' sleep. The dream was too much to get into.

"We could go to the store, I guess. But aren't you starving?"

He was trying to muster enthusiasm, but his eyes felt strained.

"Besides," she went on, bright-eyed, characteristically perky, "we have this." She swept into the breakfast nook like Loretta Young, lifted the latches, and opened the French doors on the rose garden.

"If you please." She pulled out a chair at the white table. She was not to be resisted.

Louis sat and Dana served Cap'n Crunch and instant coffee. They ate and watched the perfect morning light in the beads of dew on the pink roses and sparkling in the grass. As soon as they were finished, he retrieved the Altos map from the car.

"We just go left on Tallac Lane," he said, "then it looks like less than a mile to Lapis Lane. We turn right and take it straight into town. When do you want to go?"

"Chomping at the bit, aren't you?" She sounded testy and she knew it. They exchanged glances.

"Look, why don't you go? I'd just like to relax today, maybe get some sun. Is that okay?"

She came closer and rubbed his chest. He slipped his hand under the bottom of the nightshirt to her rear end.

"You sure? I'll miss you."

"I'll miss you too, so hurry back."

"Okay, I might as well lay in our provisions while I'm at it. Make me a list."

Louis went upstairs for his wallet and Dana wrote down whatever she could think of that seemed healthy and natural enough to suit their surroundings – various greens, whole grain bread, dark beer, chicken. She thought of couscous, realised it was probably unobtainable, and wrote down rice pilaf instead.

A few minutes later, it felt a little strange to her to be waving from the door as the Peugeot rolled down the long drive and disappeared into the trees. It was a big house,

36

very big for one person. She pushed the heavy door shut and locked it and whistled on her way back to the kitchen.

Two bowls and two cups to wash, that was it. Simplicity in the woods, Dana thought. She could live like that. She rinsed them and watched the water swirl down into the disposal. Pulverator it said on the stainless ring around the drain. It was very much like the one in their apartment, but she couldn't remember whether theirs had a name.

She rinsed faster. Silly, that's what it was. She tried to tell herself that it was, even as she watched the water make its hypnotic swirl, circling down. She always had the same feeling, even though she knew it was silly. Imagine what it would do to a hand.

Dana could almost see it – engaging the fingertips first and not letting go. It would rip in circles like a steel shark, clamped on and spinning. The rotor. If a hand slipped in, drawn by some invisible weight, a kind of compulsion . . .

It was the same again. She was starting to feel tight in the shoulders. Light-headed. It couldn't happen, not by mistake. But what if a hand were forced in somehow – seized and driven down into that loud, ripping spin? What could be done? Could you even wrench it out? Her mother was strong, she could pull the hand back. But what if you clamped her arm and kept your weight behind it, held it down with all your strength? Held it down. There would be blood, lots of it, spraying up out of the hole, speckling the enamel, and worse, bone – white splinters, cartilage, fragments pink and white . . .

Dana felt like she was being dropped. She looked into the drain and she was falling.

She reached for the faucet and shut it off matter-of-factly. She could do that and she knew all along she could. She was only playing. She shook her head briefly twice then tipped the second bowl to let the water run out and placed it upside down in the drainer.

She wasn't quite there yet, that was all. They had worked on it in therapy. It was part of a process. You couldn't separate it out from the rest. It was part of the general working-through. Dana knew she could turn it off when

37

she wanted. Her mother didn't know what Dana could and couldn't do, but Dana did.

Soon she wouldn't have to think things like that at all if she didn't want to. That was the goal, and she would reach it. She just wasn't there yet. She started upstairs and by the time she reached the landing, she realised she was whistling again.

In the bedroom she ran her fingers through her hair and shook it and checked the results in the round mirror over the dresser. Not bad. At least he hadn't thought so last night. But all cats are grey in the dark. Studying her crow's feet, Dana could almost convince herself she was looking younger, but that couldn't happen so fast. Give it a day or two. Besides, wrinkles didn't hurt Jane Fonda.

She dragged both suitcases over to the dresser, spread them open, and began to fold the rest of whatever wasn't too badly wrinkled into the deep walnut drawers. Where was an ironing board? She thought of closets she hadn't tried yet near the pantry.

Putting the clothes away reminded her of her mother again and of the phone number she had promised. It was making her nervous. Clear the mind. Open the drawer. Fold pants and lay them flat. Sachets would be nice in the drawers, she thought. She would pick up some whenever she went into town with Louis – if they had heard of them in Lapis, that is.

As she worked, Dana realised she was feeling funny again. Enough was enough, she told herself.

It would be good practice for her if she didn't even turn to look. There was no reason to. It wasn't an uncommon experience for anyone, having the peculiar sense of being stared at from behind. Just having the feeling didn't make it true. She had to grow up someday. There was an adult way to deal with this. She pictured herself turning around casually, seeing no one, turning back.

Then she remembered. Standing in the front yard, looking up. She thought something had moved beside the curtain. The bay window of the master bedroom. The eyelet curtain across the room. Behind her back.

38

Dana gasped and wheeled.

"Shit!" she screamed. The drawer had slammed on her thumb behind her.

The curtains beside both windows hung straight down. The door to the bathroom was open, and she could see that it was empty too. She was alone in the room. Dana looked at the temporary dent in her thumb then sucked it.

Morning light was flooding the windows, falling warm and bright on the quilt and the red rug. It helped to settle her down. You were supposed to be able to see the lake, she remembered. She went to the window that faced the front and looked out.

On the side of the yard opposite the driveway, there was a concrete birdbath she hadn't noticed, with two birds she guessed were wrens bobbing in it. At the end of the yard, just above the tops of the trees where the driveway disappeared, a thrilling slice of bright water was visible far down the hill.

She spotted a patch of lavender flowers between the birdbath and the woods. In the sunlight, the grass was a rich shimmering green. The summer morning was too alluring, too hard to resist even if she didn't know exactly where she wanted to go.

She unpacked in a rush and folded the rest of the clothes into the drawers fast. Then she pulled on jeans and shirt, made sure she had her keys, and locked the front door securely as she went out.

The toes of her Reeboks were wet by the time she was halfway through the yard. Ordinarily she would be at work by eight thirty, manoeuvring through the halls and cubicles of beige and grey, no morning dew in sight. She walked deliberately, deep steps, then squatted down and combed her fingers through the grass until both hands were wet. She loved the sensual smell of the moist earth beginning to warm.

She got up and went to the birdbath. Like some people, it was better from a distance. Dung-spotted around the concrete rim, it was dotted with islands of green goo in the middle, and miniature forests of algae grew up through the water. She bent over and peered in. Yuk. Maybe birds liked it that way.

Next she went to the flower patch. The lavender-coloured blooms were shaped like petunias, but she knew they weren't. She could identify a rose and a poinsettia and the common kinds of carnation and iris she took home from Safeway or the hole-in-the-wall flower shop on Sacramento Street. But if she had to tell the difference between a dahlia and a zinnia, that would be trouble. She would look in the den for a field guide to wildflowers and birds. Trees she would learn later, maybe week two. The next time they went camping, she'd know what the hell was out there. Louis would be impressed. Better yet, maybe they could learn together. Get him interested first.

She knelt and plucked a few flowers. The sun was warm on her back. Then she spotted some daisies close to the spot where the drive entered the trees. She had always liked daisies – they were handsome and honest. She crossed the end of the yard and added to the bouquet.

Dana could almost see the spot where the curving drive would meet the road. Sun was breaking through the trees just past the curve, falling at an angle on the cinders. The smells of earth and grass and woods mingled in a heady blend. Louis wouldn't be back for a while, an hour at least. It was time to explore.

She glanced back at the front of the house. From where she stood, the reflecting sun on the front of the bay window made a rectangle of solid white. She had definitely locked the front door. She raised the bouquet and sniffed a hint of sweetness. Then she entered the cool, curving driveway through the trees.

A sudden rustling to her left nearly made her jump. A wiry-looking grey squirrel regarded her from a tree trunk above the spot where it had cut a noisy trail through the leaves. She waved. Its tail waved a moment, then it froze and watched her.

Dana remembered the lake. Maybe she could see it from the end of the drive. She followed the cinder path, well worn with tyre ruts, and emerged on Tallac Lane.

40

An elevated shoulder ran between the road and a trench filled with leaves and debris, a channel for the spring run-off. She stood on the shoulder and looked south, but the lake was obscured by the trees that descended the hill on the other side of the road. She followed the shoulder to the left, in the direction Louis said he would take to pick up the road to Lapis.

As she walked, it felt like true adventure in the wild. There was a call in the woods, and she imagined it was an owl. Farther on she looked for the lake again but couldn't see it. She decided to cross the road and try to find an opening in the trees.

On the downhill side, seemingly in the midst of solitude, humans had left a trail: Coors and Bud, Diet Coke and Seven-Up cans and plastic bottles. Here and there a white styro cup had floated out of a speeding window and settled on the leaves, never to degrade, permanent as a plastic turd.

A short distance down from the road the litter disappeared and the forest took over. She stepped carefully as the way got steep then levelled. Instead of affording a better view, the trees crowded. The matting of needles and leaves underfoot was wet. There were patches where a boulder or a small slide or a fallen tree had left a brief opening, and Dana stepped around the trees gingerly to find the gaps.

Birds jabbered above her head and darted in the high branches. The underbrush grew dense, and as she worked her way down, she tried to step around all the bushes. Keep the hands off the leaves, she told herself. She might be a city rube, but she did know poison oak's reputation.

A rush in the leaves to her right wasn't frightening this time. Dana laid back part of a bush with her sleeve and peered through the hole.

She was right. A squirrel sat up on a fallen log in a small clearing, tail whipping. He was sniffing and glancing about, and his perch seemed to be the best chance for an overlook Dana had found.

The moment she stepped into the clearing, he dropped and skittered away. His log was a wide trunk, fallen with

41

the nose down but almost level with the ground. Sun was striking it from an opening and Dana was getting excited. The moss on its side and top was grey and green and made climbing on it tricky, especially with flowers in one hand.

She made sure each shoe was firmly planted then stood up. Directly in front of her, out towards the end of a branch, a blackbird was watching. Just to the left of it, a view opened through the foliage. It could almost have been man-made, a tunnel bored through the leaves. Sunlight filtered through it, and the mist in the opening glowed and glistened on the leaves, light as a halo.

It was a magical tunnel. She edged sideways a few feet for a better view. At the end of the opening, under less reflected brightness than she had seen from the bedroom window, deep blue but glitter-sprinkled with sun, lay the lake. Dana gasped when she saw it. The quality of the blue, its darkness, made it seem bottomless. What was it, a thousand feet? Nearly two thousand out there somewhere? What if you capsized in the middle and started sinking? Would you drift down for an hour or more?

The water was so beautiful, it almost seemed to beckon to her. She moved to her left a little and saw a motorboat heading out from shore trailing a white line. Something moved behind her.

At first she didn't turn. She wasn't going to be spooked by squirrels. It could even have been a bird on the ground or in a low bush, hopping through leaves. The next time it moved, she was guessing again.

It was heavier. Simply from the sound of the motion, a single step or a short movement to one side or the other in the leaves, Dana knew it was larger than a squirrel, and more than a little larger.

The Big Tree Campers lot was the first sign to Louis that he was on the main drag. Lapis appeared shortly after it, a downtown of small store fronts: an ancient saloon, a prosperous-looking hardware store, a drugstore with an old orange sign.

A car cruised out lazily from the kerb and he rolled up

42

on it too fast. Watch the road, he told himself out loud. He was feeling groggy, still in the aftermath of the dream. It was hard to shake. Real coffee was what he needed. He could have killed for a San Francisco espresso.

A sign on one of the façades a couple of blocks down caught his eye – General Store and Café. The café was what hooked him, with the taste of the thought of espresso in his mouth.

As he angled to the kerb, he was having second thoughts. There was something about the front of the place – the curtains too chintzy yellow, the walls and window trim green and brown like Lincoln Logs – that seemed self-consciously atmospheric. He was imagining gourmet coffees in little boxes. Still, it had to be better than instant. He turned the key and got out.

Louis took a deep breath and tried to wake up. It was fresh and clean and splendid in the mountains. People did make a living here, somehow. The guy he followed to the door wore a walrus moustache and a faded ZZ Top T-shirt. The work boots probably had steel toes. Louis imagined wearing ones like that, rolling logs or hefting cinder blocks around a clearing that smelled of pine chips. "Walk a Mile in My Shoes" popped into his head. Who the hell sang that? Jesus, he was getting to be a fossil. The door had no closer and he pulled it shut behind him to a little bell. That felt genuine, anyway. And there was the smell of coffee in the air. Joe South. At least the memory wasn't totally gone.

The groceries were straight ahead, and the coffee aroma came from the right. He followed it into the café with grey formica tables and red booths and a counter with stools. He thought about a booth but only one was empty, and the others were all occupied by two or more. He went to the counter and sat down a few stools from a broad back in a Corona T-shirt. He was bending the ear of the old boy on his right, lean as jerky meat and wearing a cap with a bulldog on the front tilted back on his head.

"So I take one look at these panels she put in and they're all dipsey-divey. She asks me what I'm gonna do. Now about this time I can smell it on her. I know she's

43

looped. You know well as I do what that means with Janet – "

"Featherbrain," the other said.

"Right. Like that time she wanted me to keep her birds. When she got back, she called me real late, buzzed out. Said that one had a bruise on its neck. She didn't know what killed it any more than I did. It could've caught a virus or something."

"Help you?" The waitress was standing in front of him, a hazel-eyed blonde, high-school age. Mascara. Louis flashed on mascara eyes, reddish. Foam-white lips. He cleared his throat.

"Coffee, please."

"That's all?" It sounded vaguely accusatory.

Should he have a real breakfast? Did he have time? Suddenly he missed Dana. He didn't want to spend their vacation apart from her in a podunk coffee shop. Still, he was starving. The doughnut case was directly across from his stool.

"Is that a buttermilk bar?"

She nodded. He nodded and she plunked it down on the counter – good-sized with a sugary glaze. The coffee followed and it was generic restaurant brew, but not bad at all. The caffeine and sugar were like an infusion of spirit. He thought again about getting back.

Time. What did it matter? The money didn't matter either, the fact that Dana was now taking home a bigger cheque. It had been close before. A high-school teacher's salary had never inflated their savings account.

"It's not a profession to grow old in any more," Sam Wooten had confessed at the end-of-semester cocktail hour. He was half in the bag and slurring, but the deep creases under his eyes and the cynical droop in his mouth weren't from the Scotch. Sam had had it with the macho mouths and the bullet heads and the radio salvos from the back of the classroom. He had wearied of the bone-headed, conflicted knockoffs of Prince or Death Vyper or whoever the hell it was this time around. Teaching was war without danger pay.

No profession to grow old in. If Wooten's history class wasn't, what was? Louis hadn't had the chance to find out. A year and a half ago a district budget shortfall had meant cuts, deep ones. Fewer teachers and more Apple IIs, something like that. Fewer teachers in certain subject areas, anyway, including English. At that point, holding a pink slip, he came to confront certain truths. One, he probably could have done better teaching English in Japan. Two, staying in the same field could be suicidal.

Dana always supported whatever he wanted to do whenever they had talked about it. She didn't even care about buying a house, really. It was his idea. Qualifying for a mortgage in the state of California meant a substantial two-earner income, and houses would only be more expensive the longer they waited.

So he had decided to retrain. He was on another path now, that was all – same person, new path. It would work out better in the long run, for both of them. More stability, a little disposable cash. It would make things easier for Dana. In fact, if it came down to it, that could have been what he wanted most. Things would be better. He needed to keep reminding himself.

He missed her, he realised, as he chewed and his eyes drifted over the hangings on the wall behind the counter: a Dos Equis sign, a shelf of bowling trophies, and beside the doughnut case, a photo of a man and two kids staring at a huge disc mounted on a wall. Louis squinted and made out a little of the text beside the picture. It was about calendars – Julian, Mayan, Aztec. That was the disc, a Mayan calendar. "Our days are numbered" was the caption. Don't remind me, he thought. But right they were. Everybody worried about time. So he shouldn't. He should slow down.

He unfolded the shopping list. When the waitress with the mascara eyes came by with the coffee pot, he nodded sure, why not.

Dana dropped into a crouch and stared at the spot in the woods where the sound had been. It was hard to pinpoint. The hill that rose behind her was dense with trees and brush. She leaned to one side then the other but couldn't see a thing.

She started to sit on the log for a lower view, but as she put her free hand down for balance, the mat of moss and lichens squished into a wet patch under her palm. She jerked it up instinctively, lost her balance and slipped on to her seat, skidding sideways off the log on to her hands and knees in the leaves.

It moved again, behind cover. Get back to the road. Out of the tangle of bushes and trees where you couldn't see anything, back to Tallac Lane.

Hold on. It was probably a deer. That was it, like the one they had seen from the road just past Truckee the day before. It was perfectly logical. It moved again, and as Dana listened, it kept moving.

She got up and her heart started to race. She needed to head back to the road, but the sound was above her somewhere on the hill, she was fairly sure of that. It stopped again. She listened, but whatever it was wasn't giving itself away. The bushes and trees were quiet all around her.

A dumb thought crossed her mind. It was pure Hollywood, something out of a Western or a Gordon Scott Tarzan flick. Nevertheless, it was part of her outdoor lore – maybe, if she had to be honest, the sum total of it. Where were the birds? When she listened, she heard none at all. Had she scared them off? If she hadn't, something had – something up there on the hill.

Dana ran out of the clearing into the bushes. She didn't want it to spot her in the open. She hopped over a high root and hit at an angle then caught herself against a tree, raking her knuckles and smashing the lavender flowers. She threw them down and clambered through the bushes.

She couldn't hear it any more. Why didn't it move again? At least she'd have an idea of where it was and where she was going. Keep moving. Branches grabbed her. Screw the poison oak. How far could the road be?

"Wolves. I'm telling you, they're wolves."

"There aren't any left in these parts, Mrs Cheney," the

grocer assured an elderly lady in the checkout line. Louis overheard them as he reached for the top of the paper-towel stack at the end of the aisle.

"I heard them up there, Ike. I know. One of these days, they might come down in town here where you live – late at night. It just depends how hungry they get. Mr Cheney used to say you never know what a wolf will do."

Louis saw Ike grinning at the man in line behind her, the wiry one from the counter in the bulldog cap. Mrs Cheney situated her bag in her grocery caddy and continued towards the door.

"A wolf can't be predicted. He's wild. He'll make a fool out of you. You'll see." She jabbered on through the front door and the little bell rang behind her.

"Ding a ling," the bulldog said. Ike chuckled and rang up his charcoal lighter and barbecued chips.

"They're a-stinct," the bulldog went on and Ike agreed.

Extinct or not, the wolf talk made Louis think of Dana alone in the house. Wolves didn't attack houses, did they?

He took the paper towels and added some beer to the cart and hurried to the register. He was getting worked up over nothing. It was the caffeine. And that dream. It was just time to get back, that was all.

He paid and, as he reached the front door and glanced up through the opening in the yellow chintz curtains, he saw something. A tall man was standing on the sidewalk between the store and the car. He was older – Louis could tell from the stiff look of his long, angular frame and the streaks of grey in his hair. He was just standing, staring down at the white Peugeot.

Was the car enough of an oddity in Lapis to warrant stares? Was the old guy just catching his breath? He seemed to be concentrating. Louis imagined that if he went to the car, the man would move on or talk. Why did that seem hard to do? The old character was giving him the creeps somehow. He was still on edge from the dream, he realised. He pushed the door and stepped out.

As he did, and it closed behind him, the old man turned,

as though on cue, and started down the walk in the opposite direction.

By the time Louis got the groceries into the car and started up and fastened his seatbelt, the man had vanished. He had disappeared into one of the stores along the walk; the saloon, Louis imagined. He backed up and started out of town the way he had come.

He pictured Dana in the sauna the night before, then he was thinking back to her in bed. He wouldn't mind getting home at all. He was recalling their arrival at Alpenhurst when he realised the light was red. He hit the brake and halted in the crosswalk. Louis glanced at the kerb to see if he would be blocking pedestrians, and he saw the old man again.

He was standing stiffly at the kerb, making no move to cross the street, only staring out between the white lines in the direction of the car. Louis felt his heart clutch.

A horn was blowing behind him. He checked the rearview mirror and it was full of a camper van – from Big Tree, he guessed. He glanced up at a green light.

"Shit," he said and stepped on the gas. In a few minutes Dana was slipping back into his mind, erasing all thoughts of the old man.

Dana churned up the hill, gasping for breath. It was quiet all around her and the quiet was evil.

The ground levelled and she could make time. She tore around a bush and there, on the other side, was sheer terror. She screamed.

Just beyond the shrub, it was hunching so low she almost kicked it. Even as she was trying to pull up and away, her shin struck a dull, glancing blow, and it howled.

She hit her shoulder and rolled, but not far. A bush blocked her. Was she six feet from it? Less? She could scramble on hands and knees through the roots if she had to. What had she seen behind her? Could it have been? Flat on her stomach in the dirt and pine needles, she glanced back.

Fear was powerful, Dana understood at that moment. She

had been so tuned by it, so ready, that it hadn't registered as she broke through the bush and hit and rolled. It was a man on all fours that she had seen, pulled into a crouch. He was staring at Dana wild-eyed, looking as scared as she was.

They eyed each other, frozen for a long moment, he in his crouch and Dana in her lizard pose, line of sight over her shoulder and rear end. Finally the man was laughing, beginning to rise.

"Are you all right?" he stammered. The oriental man was grinning and laughing nervously. He wore a red cap and an astoundingly loud yellow shirt with black patterns.

Dana couldn't move at all at first, or speak, but then she began to giggle and it was like a dam breaking inside. The man giggled too and he was laughing hard as he hobbled over and knelt down. Dana turned and sat up slowly, nearly debilitated by giggles.

"Okay?" the man asked solicitously. "Okay?"

Dana finally recovered enough to nod. Tears filled her eyes and her stomach hurt. The man stood up and extended his hand and she took it.

"Careful now," he said. "Careful."

She got up slowly, brushing the pine needles off her shirt. The knees of her faded jeans were dark with two childish patches of moist dirt. She tried to remember where the washing machine was. Then she remembered to feel for broken bones.

"Thanks, I'm okay," she said. "God, I'm sorry. I was down the hill and I heard something and I thought . . . I didn't know what I thought, really." He was nodding and smiling and Dana realised she was babbling. "I'm really sorry. How are *you*?"

"Oh, I'm fine. I was the one making the noise, I'm sure – "

"Oh no, it wasn't disturbing me. It's just that I don't spend much time in the woods – " He was watching her intently, grinning along.

"What I mean is, I got nervous for no reason. It wasn't your fault at all." She extended her hand. "I'm Dana Ferrin."

"Pleased to meet you. I am Kenji Sukaro."

For the first time his outfit actually registered. It was hard not to stare. The khaki pants were fairly average-looking but with complex pockets under pockets on each leg. At the ends of the legs bright red high-tops protruded. They almost but not quite matched the red cap with the black and gold "Fujitsu" emblem in the centre, gold robots tilting around it like space walkers. His bright yellow smock was covered with a smattering of black polygons.

"At least the hunters won't think I'm a deer, you know?" Not knowing what to say, Dana laughed. Was she that obvious? "You can't be too careful, I think. Especially because I spend a lot of time out here. You never know about some of these people with their guns – very dangerous." His face was roundish and cheerful and she couldn't tell whether he was serious or not.

"I'm a collector, you see," he explained. "It's my obsession, one of them, anyway." He laughed and gestured towards the bush where she had tripped over him. On the ground lay a white canvas sack with leather handles. He retrieved it and extracted something for Dana.

"Don't you have to be very careful?" She knew she knew that much.

"You do have to know what you're doing, but there aren't that many poisonous species. Most are the *Amanitas*. *Amanita verna* accounts for ninety per cent of the deaths from eating mushrooms. 'The destroying angel' they call it."

"It sounds frightful."

"Actually, most mushrooms are excellent foods, a great source of Vitamin B. This is a very common edible mushroom, *Agaricus campestris*." He rotated it between thumb and forefinger like a cocktail parasol from Trader Vic's. "You've probably seen it a thousand times."

"I think so, but most mushrooms look pretty much alike, right? That's how the poisonous ones get you."

"No, no, no. Here, you'll see the difference." He dipped back into the sack and traded his *Agaricus* for another. It was elongated, funnel-shaped and yellowish. It seemed

50

magical and cartoon-like to Dana, a treasure of the Seven Dwarfs.

"This is the lovely chanterelle – in France, a delicacy. The Roman emperors considered another, the royal agaric, to be the choicest of foods. It's very distinctive-looking, large and reddish-orange."

"A consuming passion," Dana let it slip. Kenji laughed.

"A punster after my own heart. Actually, I do find it fascinating. Of course, it is a little strange to most people, rooting around after a fungus. Mushrooms aren't plants; they don't have any chlorophyll. But people do get very interested in them. John Cage, the great composer, is a mushroom fanatic. I collected with him once." Dana nodded seriously, trying to show proper awe. Kenji nodded back.

"It sounds like fun. I've made up my mind to learn something about nature myself, now that I have the chance. There isn't much opportunity in the city."

"You're from San Francisco?"

Dana wondered how he knew, then realised it was a fairly safe guess.

"My husband and I are staying in Alpenhurst, just up the hill. We won a free month in a contest. It's so lovely."

"What good luck! My place is just down the hill. I'm having a few people over for drinks on Friday evening. I'd be so pleased if you could join us."

"That's very nice. Are you sure?"

"Definitely. It's so refreshing to see new faces. We tend to get in a rut up here, the same people at every party, you know?" Kenji was smiling, but his eyes seemed not to smile. "Like a family, we sometimes come to know one another too well."

"I'm sure we'd be happy to come. I'll check with Louis and I can phone you."

Kenji wrote his number on a small notepad from one of the mid-thigh pockets. He also drew Dana a map of the route from Alpenhurst down the Lapis Road, finally branching eastwards all the way to the lake. Then he pointed the way to a footpath she could take back uphill.

"Okay, see you, Dana," Kenji called over his shoulder as

51

he went the other way down the path. "See you Friday." He looked like a bright yellow flag of some friendly nation.

Dana soon found the shoulder of Tallac Lane and followed it in the direction of the driveway. She laughed to herself, thinking how she could recount the episode to Louis. She couldn't quite find a way to describe how Kenji's face smiled while his eyes seemed serious. But that didn't seem to be an important part of the story anyway.

7

They were on old Lapis Road, heading towards the lake. It was nearly seven, but there was still plenty of sun on the blacktop that wound through the woods.

"So what's he into besides mushrooms?" Louis asked. "It's not going to be fondue or something is it? Hundreds of mushroom caps in boiling oil . . ."

"Thousands. Here," Dana interrupted, "go right."

Kenji's map guided them on to a one-lane dirt road that snaked down the hill. Soon they were on a low ridge, and the lake appeared suddenly between the trees. Between the road and the lake an imposing split-level home swung into view, and several cars were angled into the gravel lot in front of it.

"Looks like exclusive company," Louis said as they turned and banked down the gradient. He was referring to an olive Mercedes in the lot and both of the cars in the garage, a yellow Triumph and a Porsche the colour of pinot noir.

"They're not all like that," Dana countered. A four-wheel-drive Scout and a Toyota wagon sat in the drive too, but a Saab 9000 and a BMW 320i were parked by the trees where she hadn't noticed them at first.

"Do you believe this house!" she was exclaiming, her door already open as Louis cut the engine.

It was a magnificent structure of stone and heavy timbers, contemporary but echoing the elegantly warm style of the old Tahoe houses. A curving solarium made up one entire end, and Dana saw two large skylights in the roof which seemed to be made of aluminium, shiny and steeply pitched. It was the kind of roof, built to shed the snow, they remembered from passing through Truckee. The garage was beneath the house, and just to the right, broad stone steps curved up to double doors with a pair of black ring knockers.

Dana headed for the steps and Louis followed, pushing his tie around until the knot felt straight. Her perfume smelled sweet-fresh as she reached the porch ahead of him and pressed the bell. They waited. There was faint music inside.

"I don't think they heard it." He was thinking of reaching for the knocker when the door swung open.

"Dana! Greetings, good evening. Come in, please." Kenji took her hand, all smiles. He was wearing an oversized shirt, lurid orange this time, patterns like pieces of a jigsaw puzzle that had been dropped and reshuffled randomly in layers. Gurkha shorts and hurachi sandals down below.

"Hi, Kenji. This is Louis."

As he shook Kenji's hand, Louis had the feeling that it was all a ruse. The Bonzai jester outfit and the toothy smile. There was a firmness in his look as he shook hands. It had nothing to do with a macho grip. His handshake wasn't so strong at all. It didn't have to be, that was the point. Don't underestimate him.

"Your house is lovely," Dana was saying. Fusion jazz was coming from everywhere and nowhere in particular, covering the conversations in the living room. A cathedral ceiling zoomed above them, at least twenty feet at the highest point. A skylight was situated so that, late at night, anyone on the huge white leather sectional in the middle of the room would look up into a ceiling of stars.

Most of the dozen or so guests in the room were clumped around the sectional, and beyond them a massive stone fireplace, open-hearth, occupied much of the far wall. A few other guests were standing just to the left of the living room in front of a broad picture window, and Kenji was heading towards them.

"Whit," he called to a stocky back. The man was standing, drink in hand, looking out at the lake. "I'd like you to meet two new friends."

At first he looked surprised, shocked out of deep thoughts, then it was clear that he was naturally bug-eyed. As they were introduced, Whit Norwood's eyes narrowed in a curious way, as though taking a close reading of each of them, but just for a moment. When he spoke, it was directed at Kenji.

"Is that a shirt or a call to arms?"

Kenji broke up. Whit's mouth snapped into a sideways, cranked-up smile then back to its natural froglike state, lips compressed into a line and lower jaw out. He wasn't finished. "It's about as subtle as Gorgonzola cheese."

They were all laughing so he smiled again and left the crooked smile on for a while. He looked like a precocious kid, finished with his performance and proud of himself. His eyes were the colour of bourbon, and Dana noticed the network of tiny red veins in his nose. A beer belly strained his Omaha Beach Club T-shirt to tautness. Thumping it would make a watermelon sound. His neck was short and bullish, and smiling made his face redder.

"We always count on Whit for an encouraging word," Kenji added.

"You wanna see me do my thang," Whit twanged, "pull my strang." His face reverted to a cynical frog's.

"Whit was an animator for the Disney studios for several years. He worked on *Peter Pan* and quite a few others. How many times did you draw the crocodile?"

"Around fifty thousand, give or take ten thousand. The croc with the tick-tock clock." Whit raised his glass in salute then drained the Scotch from the ice.

"We must toast the croc – forgive me," Kenji apologised for the lack of drinks. "Kizzie! Kizzie!" he called and waved someone over from the living-room crowd.

A blonde girl in a faded denim jacket and short leather skirt strolled towards them with a tray of wines – some red, some white, champagne and two that looked like sherry. The jacket had been customised with studs and sequins

54

and two multi-coloured tassels, one on the front of each shoulder. Her hair looked fried with platinum, and her eyes had a "fuck you" Hollywood Boulevard look, but her mouth held a lazy smile. On her left breast it said "Kizmet" in silvery studs.

"The real booze is over here," Whit announced, pointing towards the liquor caddy at the far end of the curving window. "He keeps it hidden as long as he can."

"This is fine," Dana said as she took a white from the tray. Louis took a red. "The crocodile with the tick-tock." She raised her glass.

"The croc," the others toasted. Whit raised his glass but got only ice on the upper lip and a trickle of cold water.

"Oh well," he said, "most toasts are a crock, anyway."

They all chuckled then fell silent for a moment.

"Quite a lake," Louis ventured, then realised how inane it sounded.

"It's glorious," Dana added. "How long until sunset?"

"Any minute," Kenji said.

It was a stunning view. On the vast sheet of nearly flat water, the sundown light made a deep metallic orange-red. The picture window was built in segments, tall panes joined by redwood cornices, tilting outwards so that the tops were over the water. They met at angles, forming the curving window that ran the width of the wall. It afforded a panoramic view of Lake Tahoe. The far shore couldn't be distinguished, but close to the house the treetops formed a jagged black line in the evening light and threw long shadows on the surface.

"It has been said," Whit began, "by those luminaries born to calculate such things, that if you spilled Lake Tahoe on to California, it would cover the entire state to a depth of more than a foot, with an average lake or two left over. Keep it in mind if you get the urge to upend the lake while you're here." He pulled a half-crushed pack of Camels out of his shirt pocket and extracted one with his lips.

"What brings you to our little enclave, if I may be . . ."

Whit smashed the end of his nose with his finger, "blunt?"
Kizmet giggled.

Dana told him about the contest and Alpenhurst. Whit
remarked that he knew the house well, that he and his wife
had spent a nice summer with a couple named Rose four
years ago. The Norwoods had dined in the house often that
year. Although the Roses had purchased a share, and the
couples made plans to meet again the next summer, they
failed to reappear, and their time slot was filled by three gay
men. A letter to their home in Los Angeles was returned,
so Whit theorised they moved, or there had been a death.
A pause seemed to be waiting for someone to change the
subject.

"Do you still draw?" Louis asked.

"I'm retired."

"He draws," Kizmet protested. "He does cartoons for
the *Bay View*. They're so wacked out, I love them."

"Grr," Whit replied, "come with me and be mine." Kizzie
pecked him on the jowl.

"Later, gator," she said and toured off with her tray,
joining up with an oriental girl in a short black dress and
tights and red shoes.

"So how do you like it up here?" Dana asked. "It's pretty
far from Hollywood."

"Heaven on earth, as long as you like trees. Would you
believe you can get bored with all this? And Lapis, there's a
town. Been there yet? You can always tell a tourist in Lapis
– he'll be the one wearing shoes. Ellie loves it, though. She
can actually find things to do. You can get all the social
dirt from her."

Whit glanced towards the living room, and Dana thought
he looked nervous. She followed his glance but couldn't spot
the target at first. Then a blonde with high hair waved a
little toodle-loo wave in their direction. She looked fifteen
years younger than Whit. Then Dana realised that a lot
of makeup and Whit's dissipation probably accounted for
most of the difference.

Dana looked back and caught him blowing a little kiss of
recognition with his cigarette hand. He was nervous about

56

something, all right. Was it the dark-haired guy she was talking to?

"Let me introduce you," Kenji offered.

"Nice to see you, folks," Whit said, lighting up and dragging deep. "I go to replenish." He hoisted his glass. "In honour of the dying day, which is not even 'colourised'." Smoke trailed out of each nostril, but very little.

Louis and Dana followed Kenji in the direction of Whit's wife. She was wearing a coral evening gown, long and cut straight across the bust. It could have been a hip takeoff on the fifties, but Dana didn't think so. They exchanged pleasantries with Ellie Norwood and the man beside her. Dana's curiosity was satisfied – she introduced Lloyd Burris, the sheriff of Lapis.

"Was Whit filling you full of his usual nonsense?" she asked.

"Your husband is charming," Dana said. "Does he keep you laughing at home?"

"Sporadically. After twenty-three years that must mean something. What, I'm not sure. What about you two? How long have you been married?"

Dana liked talking with her. Her face was roomy and she had an easy, accepting way, but with a hint of firmness underneath. Dana imagined Ellie had suffered in her life, and probably more than once. She could have been early to mid-fifties, about ten years younger than Whit. She also had good bones and held herself well, and Dana fantasised they had met in Hollywood and that Ellie had been a stunner in her day.

Louis felt easy with her too. There was something touching about her, a little sad, like her mixed aromas of perfume and bourbon. Maybe she wanted to think of them as kids. He hoped Dana didn't go overboard. She was always looking for a mother figure, even though she'd deny it. If he had Dana's mother, he thought, he'd look for another one too.

"So, what kind of trouble do you get up here? It's hard to imagine any." Louis turned to Lloyd Burris as Ellie and Dana chatted.

"Prowlers, break-ins." Lloyd was tall and rangy, a Dennis Weaver build. He couldn't have been much over thirty. "There are quite a few nice houses up here. People leave them unattended a lot of the time. It's like an invitation. Then you've got a lot of local entrepreneurs. Weed ranchers, know what I mean?"

Louis nodded, wondering if he busted the marijuana farmers with one of the four-wheels in the lot outside or if he flew in a chopper brigade, the kind they used in Mendocino County. He was young but his eyes were cool, oyster-grey. Louis felt the sheriff sizing him up, and there was something in the look he didn't care for.

"So how do you know he was the right one?" interrupted over Louis's shoulder.

"Because," the voice sounded young and blasé, "he never laughs at the right things. He's so great."

Louis had to turn. It was Kizmet's oriental friend. Over her black dress she wore a vest fashioned of a material like chain mail. She took a drag on a cigarette and the air smelled heavily of cloves.

The girl was talking to a middle-aged woman in country-casual suede and huge designer frames with pink lenses. Her face looked leatherised from all-season leisure in the sun. On her finger she wore a rock like the Ritz, and Louis imagined Tahoe was a temporary stopover between Aspen and Palm Springs.

He glanced around the room. What an odd crowd. It reminded him of a sixties album cover – *Sergeant Pepper* or *The Band* – with everybody's weird friends and relations in the shot around the stars. He wondered who the stars of this performance were.

"How are we doing?"

Louis almost jumped. Kenji had slipped back in behind him. He realised he was annoyed and tried not to show it – the oily social "we" always set him off. It sounded condescending and unctuous, like something an activities director might say. But as he tried to nod pleasantly, he sensed something more. It was oddly familiar at first, disconcerting. Then he made the connection. Even as Kenji

58

was smiling, something was cooling his eyes, slackening the muscles around them. Louis checked himself. Was he still unnerved by Lloyd's cool stare or were their eyes really similar, noncommittal and distant even as they seemed to be behaving cordially? Kenji disrupted the thought.

"You must have a good job to be able to take off a month of summer."

"I'm in mortgage brokerage." It still sounded like a confession when he said it, as though he were talking about somebody else.

"Ah!" Kenji exclaimed, sounding thrilled, a stupefying notion to Louis. "A business tied to the fluctuating barometer of interest rates."

"I guess you could say that."

"Come with me," he said. Kenji turned and headed in the direction of the door. His dark eyes swivelled like a hook, and Louis was following. At the end of the foyer, curving stairs rose into shadows, carpeted in burgundy and dimly lighted.

"I'm going to tell Noah when he comes." A woman with hair cut in a tight dome like feathers was descending, talking over her shoulder. Her companion, frizzy-haired, in a crocheted blouse and clogs, followed closely. Louis caught the snatch of conversation as they passed. Kenji was climbing without looking back.

"Are you sure . . .?" the other woman said before the voices were out of earshot. A few more steps and he joined Kenji on the landing.

The hall curved like a wide balcony. Kenji was gliding ahead. Their footsteps made no sound on the carpet. Music was coming softly from ceiling speakers and voices bubbled from below. They passed a closed door. Louis had a strangely dizzy feeling looking down on the guests. He tried to spot Dana, but Kenji was opening a second door. He turned with a cat's grin and watched Louis as he came closer.

Inside, an unearthly green emanation lighted an otherwise dark room. The light fell from computer screens, three arranged in a semicircle, a printer attached to one and a

59

device like a small photocopying machine to another. On the monitors, line graphs were displayed like mountain ranges in green phosphor.

"These are my lifelines," Kenji explained. "I make my living in the commodities markets. With these I keep a watch on prices and make my own trades. No middle man." The smile seemed never to leave his face, it only modulated. It became contentment.

"Excellent," Louis said. "Nothing like being your own boss."

What was he talking about? he grilled himself. He had no idea what being your own boss was like. His dad had owned a foundry in Chicago, maybe that was experience enough to speak from. No, he was mouthing platitudes. Just bullshit.

"This one monitors T-bill trading only, and it's fascinating, the correlation you can see on hard copy between interest rates . . ." Kenji reached behind the printer and began sorting through the paper that had piled up during the trading day.

Louis felt envy beginning to build. That was how he did it – the house and the cars. That was the secret behind his in-charge attitude, a foundation of wealth, burgeoning even as they stood there in front of the hills and valleys in the graphs, each change in direction representing an opportunity to make more money, to get freer. He had done it his own way, often enough that now he answered to no one.

Kenji was demonstrating on the printout how interest rates influenced the prices of lumber and gold futures. Louis focused on the dull, enervating experience of going to his desk in the morning and answering the first phone call. It was depressingly void, but listening to Kenji was getting him oddly excited. It seemed to carry a promise of some kind, a hope of a way out. But how could it be for him? That wasn't clear. Still, it might not be impossible. There was a difference between impossible and not extremely likely, wasn't there? Fortunately, yes. Louis smiled and nodded.

60

Kenji pressed two keys on one of the keyboards then pointed to the areas of the screen that showed the margin money required to purchase a contract. Louis compared the data closely to the lines which would begin to creep slowly across the screens, updating in real time, when the trading day began in London. He started to raise his glass then realised it was empty and tried to concentrate on Kenji's every word. Maybe he could understand just enough. Maybe understanding was the way in.

"Charming earrings, dear," Ellie was saying.

"They're from Asenza," the woman replied.

"That's one of the places I was telling you about," Ellie explained to Dana. "It's in Carnelian Bay."

"They're lovely," Dana rather forced herself to say. The older woman struck her as cool and aloof. The earrings looked like bugs of some kind. "What are they made of?"

"Lapis, actually," the woman replied. "Local colour." She allowed a trace of a smile and it almost seemed like a mistake.

Ellie had introduced Frieda Beckman as a friend in her embracing way, but Dana found it hard to imagine that they had much in common. Frieda was older, around sixty-five, but she seemed concerned to project greater age and profound wisdom. It was an aura that may have accounted for her success, Dana imagined, or possibly it was the other way around.

Frieda was an analyst, semi-retired, dividing her time between Tahoe and a home in Tiburon. Dana knew Tiburon, the little peninsula community which extended into the bay near Sausalito. Old and rich. Very. She pictured Frieda Beckman moving in another world, wives of financiers and corporate counsels who desired, as one more self-enrichment activity like learning to cook Thai, to engage in a decade of soul-baring and who could pay the price.

"What style of therapy do you practise?" She felt she knew enough to ask that.

"Jungian analysis," Frieda replied, nodding, without

61

explication. Either you knew it or you didn't. Dana remembered the name from college and nodded back, having no idea what to say next.

Conveniently, Ellie began just then to relate a dream that had been puzzling her. Dana had a moment to study the analyst, examine the cool surface, alluring as platinum. Like the blue earrings, the rest of the outfit was eminently tasteful, a tan St Tropez-style summer dress and long grey shirt vest. Dana was surprised to admit it to herself, but she was more at ease with Ellie's fragile charm. She did admire the woman, though, she could certainly say that, especially the quiet power behind the grey eyes. She glanced back at the earring. It was a mantis. A praying mantis, wasn't that it? An insect that devoured its young?

Ellie had finished her dream, a sojourn in a bus station in the South and an encounter with a young porter and an old station master. Frieda had expressed interest, but now she was looking back at Dana in a thoughtful way that was making her feel like a fish in a tank.

She glanced around the floor, looking for Louis. Whit was standing with another group by the window, and she spotted Lloyd Burris by the fireplace listening to a woman in a sixties-style crocheted blouse. A whiff of panic went through her. Had he left?

The old woman was giving her a pain. She could learn to keep those all-knowing eyes to herself, that brittle stare. Dana might just snap it. She might break it off so fast . . . No. There would be none of that now.

She looked up just as Louis appeared behind the rail on the second-floor landing. Kenji was behind him.

The cave of the monitors, he was thinking as he stepped out of the green room and glanced down on the crowd and on Dana waving. What was up? Ellie Norwood waved too and Louis raised his empty glass. What did they want? He had a funny feeling about it as he and Kenji headed back towards the stairs.

As they started down, he wanted to get in one more question, about extrapolating long-term trends from the

62

data. He framed it carefully in his mind, still picturing the three monitors and the graphs, the lifelines, imagining connecting with the network. Suddenly Kenji raised his hand.

They were almost halfway down the stairs, just far enough to have an angle on the open front door and a new guest standing in the hall.

"Who – ?"

"Noah. Noah Taggart," Kenji said, and Louis remembered the woman mentioning the name on the stairs. "He lives in Dunn's Crest, up the hill from you."

Louis looked down on him from above, a tall, angular figure, shoulders hunching slightly forwards, long hair combed straight back, mostly black but streaked with grey. Someone he had seen before.

By the time they reached the bottom of the stairs, the man had stepped into the living room, and the other guests had drawn in, surrounding him. He could have been a sitcom star, Louis thought. He did seem a little glum for it, mouldy around the edges. Maybe he was Timothy Leary come back from the bottomless graveyard of the out-of-vogue. He seemed older than Tim Leary, but it was hard to place his age exactly. The eyes around Taggart were fixed, glued to the subject. Whatever it was, Taggart had it, x-factor, the thing that made you tune in.

It wasn't the way he dressed, although the clothes were far from ordinary. They were understated and fine – the greyish tweed jacket and the starch-collared linen shirt. His silk ascot had golden browns in it and a shade of violet that harmonised with his skin, its nearly ashen tone, and hinted at the steel-coloured hair.

Maybe it was his voice. Louis could only catch snatches of it, low and smooth, and his words, the little he could hear of them, seemed placed, not self-consciously, but in the precise way that seemed to suggest English as a third language or a fourth. It was a deep voice with a trace of an accent Louis couldn't quite identify over the distance. Everyone around him was seduced into quiet attentiveness. The sacerdotal air of the whole thing made Louis queasy, a similar feeling to the last time he had seen the man, standing like a scarecrow at the crosswalk in downtown Lapis.

"He's an interesting fellow," Kenji added. "Made his money in the mining business, diamonds, years ago. He's been around the world several times. Also became an expert mountaineer, made several Himalayan climbs. That would be enough for most people, you know?" Kenji laughed. "Not Noah. He sails too. In the Pacific he led expeditions to islands that hadn't been mapped. You should see his photos. Maybe you will – I'll introduce you." He began to work his way around the circle, holding his glass high, looking for a space to break in.

Louis suddenly realised that Kizmet was standing beside him with her tray. The three rhinestone studs in her ear increased in magnitude towards the bottom of the pink lobe.

"He's like a star, isn't he?"

She looked up at him, mascara orbs.

"Noah Taggart, I mean. He's kind of a local celebrity."

Kizmet's look seemed to say, You laugh, but I don't laugh. She extended her tray. He put his empty glass down and took another red. She gave Louis one more dark glance then moved away across the room. He watched her glide towards the far end of the window and a door he guessed led to the kitchen. She balanced the tray, pacing like a dreamer down her tunnel of silences. He had a sudden weird urge to follow. Instead he glanced back and spotted Dana.

She was standing only a few feet in front of Taggart, directly across from him among the guests. Louis tried to remember where she had been when she had waved, curious whether she had joined the groupies or whether the crowd had simply moved in her direction and stopped before the sofa. He couldn't quite remember; she might have followed Ellie because they were still together. He tried to catch her eye, but she seemed intrigued with the old man.

Taggart, who as far as Louis could tell, had made no overtures since his arrival, only responding to others, was speaking to someone. Louis thought he could have been watching Interesting Woman of the Year. He smiled to himself, but the smile was nervous. Taggart had stepped forwards and extended his hand and Dana had taken it.

She had been watching for Louis to appear in the foyer at the foot of the stairs when the door had opened. The tall man who entered looked to her like a stern classics professor stepping in from a primitive stage, a background of darkening trees around him in the open door.

Just as he came in, the conversation around Dana broke off and several people started moving towards the door. Then a hand took her just above the elbow. When she turned, Dana saw that Frieda Beckman had Ellie's arm too and was ushering them both forwards.

"It's Noah Taggart," Frieda whispered. There was something new in her eyes, a spark of excitement, almost childlike. It was that which Dana found upsetting, more than the hand on her arm. She tried to dismiss the feeling because she didn't have time to sort it out. In a moment most of the guests in the room had congregated behind the sofa, in front of the old man, and Dana found herself between Ellie and Frieda, not six feet from Noah Taggart.

"Welcome. We were beginning to wonder," Frieda said coyly and extended her left hand. She kept hold of Dana's arm with her right.

"Hello, Frieda," he said and raised her hand to his lips. "Cease your wondering, about me anyway."

He seemed cordial enough, Dana thought. His clothes were impeccable, and he did have breeding, that was obvious. It shouldn't be so surprising that Frieda had a thing for him – most of the others seemed to want to be noticed by him for some reason. But why didn't she let go of her arm? Maybe she should say something. Maybe pulling away a little would be enough. As she was about to try it, Taggart's gaze shifted away from Frieda and fastened on Dana.

"This is Dana Ferrin, Noah," Frieda said and released her arm.

"My pleasure. I understand you're staying at Alpenhurst."

He was bending forwards a little, but Taggart was still tall enough that Dana had to look up as he spoke. The eyes

65

weren't truly black, she noticed; they were deep brown but seemed black under his brows that grew dark and dense towards the inside but grey where they peaked towards the ends. His face could have been sculpted from granite, long and craggy, chipped-looking, with deep creases from his nose to the corners of his mouth and a squarish jaw and chin flecked with small scars, like the hull of an old freighter. Grey curly sideburns grew to the bottoms of his ears, and his long hair worn straight back seemed wild and romantic. Finally she saw his hand.

"Yes, hello. I am. That is, we are, my husband and I." She took his hand and he shook hers, deliberately but gently in his large hand that was still cool from the evening air. She wondered how he knew and was about to ask then realised that Kenji must have told him.

"I live up the hill from you. In fact, we may be less than two miles apart as the crow flies, but the way between our houses is long and circuitous. In this place one becomes dependent on the personalities of the various mountain roads. Your way of travelling eventually conforms to the physical way. To reach one's goal quickly comes to seem less important."

Dana felt quietened listening to him. There was an entrancing slow heaviness in his speech, and his words seemed so well chosen. He was saying effortlessly exactly what he meant.

He shook her hand again as he talked, as if to confirm his point, and at first the gesture was as reassuring as the sound of his voice. Then, as he held fast to her hand, Dana associated it with Frieda Beckman's hold on her arm, and she had a sudden irrational sense that she had been passed from hand to hand.

Again she thought of pulling away, even if gently, but as she listened to his voice, with the hint of the accent that was neither English nor Irish as she might have expected, she was soothed by it, persuaded to leave her hand where it was. In fact, when he had finished talking and their hands did part, Dana did not know whether he or she had been holding at the last.

66

"Greetings, my friend!" Kenji stepped in behind him, his hand appearing on Noah's shoulder. In the instant that Dana saw him, he was addressing himself to Noah but looking Dana squarely in the eye, and his glance felt cold. Was he jealous of the older man's attention? The next moment he and Noah were shaking hands warmly.

"Have I missed your sunset completely?" Taggart said.

"We held it for you," Kenji said pointing towards the window, beginning an exodus of the living-room crowd. The pink sundown had left a wake of burnt orange and dark violet, like a glow from an ancient forge.

"He's handsome, isn't he? I mean he has rugged good looks." Dana realised Ellie was whispering to her. "I like that in a man, don't you?"

They were behind Taggart now, as Kenji was leading him to the window. He seemed to Dana like a great black bird. Frieda Beckman and Whit Norwood stood side by side in front of the glass. Where was Louis?

She had lost him again. He had been with Kenji but he wasn't now. She glanced around the anonymous heads and finally spotted him off to the side, watching her. He seemed faraway. What was he thinking? He raised his glass and smiled. Dana blew him a kiss. It was recognition that, for Louis, it was the right distance. Wherever hoopla was, there he did not want to be also. She knew that.

"Oooh, look!" a woman's voice rose from the window.

"They're beautiful, strange but beautiful," Ellie said as Dana saw the small forms darting in formation like fish through the shadowy depth on the other side of the window.

"Bats," a man said, and Dana heard a caught breath and a giggle in the group.

"Quick devils, ain't they?"

"Radar . . ."

"I think they're creepy."

"There is a time," Taggart spoke deeply from the middle of the group, "for all creatures . . . so they say."

Dana had just blown him a kiss when Louis heard somebody mention bats. Everyone seemed excited and stepped up to his end of the window for a better look.

He did see them as they banked up and away from the glass, passing against the light from the room. Then Taggart said something and there was silence for a moment. His face from the side looked fashioned of a material more resilient than flesh, something like tusk ivory. The bats darted around and were gone.

Kenji handed Taggart a glass of champagne. As most of the guests turned back into the living room, Louis watched the old man. He seemed to be concentrating, staring out over the water where the bats had gone. It was the way he had looked on the sidewalk in Lapis. What was he doing still standing there, waiting for them to come back or acting as though he could still see them? He couldn't, Louis thought, that was for sure. Outside the warmly lighted room, beyond the tilted windows, sunset had pulled down like a shade, and the lake was a black sheet.

"I knew you'd have fun," Dana said, one hand on her dresser, stepping out of the green dress. She looked good in her black slip, and he wasn't going to argue. He was feeling okay, he had to admit, after the wine and a brandy by the fire. It also felt good to get his shoes off.

He crossed the bedroom to her and she turned and put her head down, presenting the back of her pearl necklace. He undid it, then ran his tongue along her neck and up towards her ear. She giggled and shimmied against his pants, cool silk and warm back against his bare chest.

"So when's the big expedition?" She was referring to the later part of the evening, when he and Lloyd Burris started talking about fishing. Lloyd was a trout-fishing fanatic with a boat, and he invited Louis for a trip. They even got Whit Norwood in on the plans after a few choice words on "sportfishing" for rainbows that were shorter than a dinner plate. Fishing was Louis's one redneck passion, and Dana thought it was charming.

"Why, do you want to come?" he asked.

"Could be," she purred and turned in his arms until she was facing him.

68

"Well, not now," he said. They kissed, teasing, then hotter, and he reached for the light.

From the second-floor bay window, light threw a pool over the shrubs against the house and on to the dark lawn. When the light was killed, the pool vanished. From the bushes at the edge of the yard, in the cool moist air, eyes were looking on. A tongue clicked lightly against the roof of a mouth, a small hollow sound, then again and again with a steady rhythm not unlike the ticking of a clock. The eyes watched, entranced, first the uniform blackness of the grass, and then the dark window casement.

8

"They were a pretty odd crew."

"No odder than you," Dana responded. Louis pulled the front door shut and they went down the steps in the warm sun to the car.

The day after Kenji's party had started late. In three days at Alpenhurst, Dana still hadn't seen the homely charms of Lapis. Louis was eager to show her, so they started with breakfast there in the Shutters Restaurant. By noon they had followed the winding line of rental scooters and campers all the way to King's Beach. In an open patch of sand they unfolded the ultimate indulgence Dana had discovered in the laundry room: lounge chairs.

"Want to take a dunk?" Louis pulled off his rugby shirt and put his sunglasses back on. Behind him the lake looked magnificently blue and sparkling bright. Power boats raised rooster tails of white water farther out.

"I want to toast some first, then go in and cool off. Will you go in with me again later?"

"Sure, I'll turn into a prune. No problem."

He pecked her on the cheek and strode through the soft white sand towards the shoreline. She watched him go in his orange and purple surfer trunks. He turned and waved and she waved, then he waded in to the knees and splashed water on himself. She grinned. Modern man encounters the elements. She watched him make it as far as the waist. It looked chilly, even in July. The lake must have been a huge refrigerator out there, so deep, so cold.

Dana was glad to be warm, and she was getting warmer. The sun was in perfect tanning position. She pulled off her shirt then decided to sit down before working the jeans off. She knew the beer belly on her left was ready to ogle, and she didn't want to feel self-conscious. Then she didn't care; it was a small thrill in his small life. Besides, she might want to look once or twice herself, depending on the guy. They were all around, but they were only window dressing, pleasant diversions.

She slipped her jeans down and stepped out. Then she fished the Bain de Soleil out of the beach bag and started with the arms and shoulders. Louis was swimming towards a raft anchored a way offshore. She watched him stroking with head above water, keeping his glasses dry.

She laughed. She was thinking of him insisting on buying two papers that morning, not just the little Lapis weekly, but the *San Francisco Chronicle* too, so she could check the baseball scores. She was a longtime Detroit fan, as long as she could remember, at least since Joe Pelosi took them all to see the Tigers when they were kids. She thought of her dad teaching her how to throw. It had been at the lake, that's why she was thinking of him – lying beside a lake again brought it all the way back. Joe showed her how to hold the rubber ball, fingers on the imitation seams. She remembered his index finger, the short nail, the end of it taken by some machine. Mama had outlived him.

Dana took a breath and practised shutting her mind for a moment. She concentrated on Louis. Soon her skin was shiny everywhere above and below the two black strips of her suit. She laid her head back and closed her eyes and let the sun soak in.

Even through her sunglasses and closed lids the sunlight was a bright presence, slightly reddish. Against that background, images of the beach continued to drift by: the fat man, kids ganging into the bright lake and splashing

70

and the water like diamonds in the air, Louis swimming towards the raft, a canoe gliding just beyond it and red and white and yellow sails belling out farther from shore over the deep blue.

The sun baked in. It was the most relaxed she could remember being. She took off her glasses to avoid tanning like a raccoon. What about skin cancer? Holes in the ozone layer? Ask me later. None of that applied, only the personal movies shown on the eyelids. Images of the beach merged into thoughts of Lapis.

She liked the town, actually, even though it seemed almost aggressively rustic. She didn't know precisely why, but it was hard to feel completely comfortable in any place so out of the way. She didn't know from any personal experience that small towns, behind their sleepy looks and slow greetings and gentle pace, could hide small fears and attitudes that ran deep and poisonous. It was just a feeling, a sense that she was a stranger there and would do well to remember it.

But it was charming, she could go that far. They had sat at a table for two in one of the front windows of the Shutters. Directly across the street Conroy's looked like a classic movie saloon in a Western gunfight town. At the top of the square façade was a weather-beaten plaque: 1893. Kneiper's Rexall Drugs on the corner occupied an imposing granite structure, a bank building in the days of the Comstock Lode.

"You okay?"

Her eyes popped open. Nobody there.

"You okay?" she heard Louis ask again. It was different from just remembering. His voice sounded as clear as if he had been standing beside her on the beach instead of sitting out there on the raft, somewhere on the other side of the blinding reflection. She was fighting the memory of him asking as clearly as she could hear his voice and, at first, as she surfaced out of the drowsiness from the narcotic sun, trying to concentrate, she didn't know why.

A moment later it was clear. The association returned with his voice, like a dull weight in her insides. They were at the table in the Shutters, and when he had asked it, Dana was looking shaky. She knew it, and that bothered her nearly as much as what she had been thinking.

She fought it. She tried not to let it take her. She tried to clear her mind of Louis's voice and the look of concern in his eyes, and most of all, of the Jean Risker episode.

It was more than an annoyance. It was a disturbing sign that important battles were not yet being won. The evidence was indisputable, conclusive as her quickening pulse while the images came again like a slideshow, mental snapshots of her boss's office.

Dana closed her eyes. Fight it every inch. Christ. She didn't mind comparing herself to Jesus Christ. She had thought it more than once, ever since she read that novel about Jesus having visions and dreams as a little boy. Blinding headaches. Disturbances. It turned out that they were all premonitory, a set-up for everything that was to come. He had no idea at the time that he was special – fingered, as it were, by God. Have mercy upon us.

Resist. Reject every picture that was displayed in the brain as vividly as bright water. Control the thoughts, that was the battle, the very old battle. To Dana, it was everything. But her hands were sweating. She was losing, just as she had lost at the breakfast table. She was sick at herself. She was an addict. She was giving in.

She saw herself at work again, walking down the patch between the grey and beige partitions, past the plants tied upright in their pots, leaves flopping down like shiny green tongues. It was all quite clear.

She tapped on the door jamb and Jean Risker looked up. Ann Taylor, Dana thought when she saw the bulky knit blouse, white and cocoa, shoulders padded square. Or maybe Perry Ellis. A broad leather sash belt showed above the desk, round gold buckle the diameter of a softball. A necklace trailed a wide swoop like a comet up towards the ear. Dana was holding the form of a smile.

"Sorry, do you have a minute?" she started, knowing as she said it that "sorry" was wrong. What would have been better? A million things would have been better. She tried

72

to look relaxed while curling her toes and grinding them into the sole of one shoe.

"Sure." Jean Risker sat up, the department director tuning in. Dana noticed her wrinkles. Too many tans. Straight dark hair ended above the shoulders, razor-straight on the ends, no renegade hairs, only cooperative ones.

"I just wanted to tell you . . . and ask you something. Louis and I won a contest last night, sort of a vacation . . ."

Risker raised her eyebrows and pursed her lips.

"Personnel says I have twelve vacation and four and a half personal days accrued. I know it's a little long, but I'd like to take the vacation and three of the personals."

Dana saw Risker's eyes narrow slightly. Behind them she was processing. The circuits were shuffling electrons back and forth under the skin.

"When?" Risker spoke the word and her lips met again in a thin line.

"The free month starts July 1st," Dana said. "It's earlier than we'd like, but it's the only time they had open."

Jean Risker sat back and an audible sound of annoyance came out of her nose. Her eyes looked different, tin-coloured. Dana knew it, she was tin inside. Risker was making the change before her eyes. She had tried to hide it, especially as a kid. Tin mommy, tin daddy. Jean Tin Tin.

"You're right," Dana's boss said, "three weeks is long. Have a seat."

Dana sat down in the armless chair that was just a little lower than the other. On the desk, a picture of the husband caught her eye. In a blue jogging suit he was taking short strides down a leafy hill, grinning, wholesome and beefy. The photo was turned sideways just enough to be seen, like proof.

"Where are you on Helix?"

"There's a meeting at one today. I'm sure the mailing will be – "

"The mailing is only a part, a small part. We have a launch. The POP materials have slipped over a week, I understand."

73

"That was because PD missed the target, but Production said they can get the days back – "

"We are taking this deadline very seriously, Dana. This is what I need from you. One, all the Helix POP through separations. Two, all newsletter copy approved and proofed in PageMaker files. Three, the press release on the 3.0 upgrade . . ."

Dana listened and nodded. Why hadn't she brought a yellow pad to make notes? The mouth was moving and Dana was acknowledging the sounds. Risker stopped and her eyebrows went up.

"You'll have it," Dana promised, imagining she could handle everything the boss could have said.

"Good."

She waited for more, but nothing was forthcoming. That was it, approval without approval. Take it.

"Thanks." Dana brightened, got up, and moved to the door. "I'll draft a memo for you on the days, including the jobs I need to finish between now and then."

Risker said nothing, not even an "Okay, fine". She looked down for an instant then up. Then her eyes seemed to drift out of focus and her line of sight slipped to the side into a vague look of dismissal.

Dana heard a small sharp whack like a pebble on plastic. Then there was a little cloud like a puff of white makeup settling on the top of the PC monitor on the side of Risker's desk. The boss was staring at the wall somewhere to the right of Dana's arm. She hadn't noticed the white chunk that had bounced off her monitor and landed beside her waste basket. Dana looked up.

The ceiling above the boss's desk was cracking. Thin fissures were webbing the plaster, breaking it into separate polygons, outlining jagged chunks like pieces of dry riverbed. Inside the ceiling there was a sudden sound like cracking bones. White powder spilled down from the cracks.

Plaster pebbles were hitting the centre of Risker's desk, bouncing off the monthly orders report she had been reading when Dana came in. The boss was staring into space.

74

Several chunks fell at once. One hit the husband's photograph, and it flipped off the desk, face-down on to the carpet.

Above Risker's head the ceiling began to creak and heave. There was a straining sound in the space above it, below the upper floor. Somehow there was too much pressure, too much load. The ceiling was groaning.

In the next instant it all came down in a rush that seemed like the sky breaking up and crashing in a choking cloud of white dust. The first sprinkles of powder had coated Jean Risker's perfect half-dome of hair like a strange, chic flocking. The chunks that followed hammered it. She tried to stand as plaster crashed down on her shoulders. One chunk glanced off her nose and a scream jammed in her throat. The scarf and blouse were white with chalk.

A heavy block hit her shoulder and fractured, driving her straight down into the chair. Her hands were in her eyes and she began to choke and gag. Dana was safe in the doorway, rooted to the spot. Blood was running from Risker's nose.

Littered with plaster, the desk was beginning to vibrate. Dust was rising from it. The legs were bouncing on the floor, as if a powerful hand had it from behind and was shaking it like a rattle.

Then it was as though a driver mistook the gas for the brake. Or maybe the car and twenty thousand like it should have been recalled but weren't and the transmission had popped from neutral into reverse. Jean Risker's desk suddenly accelerated backwards, taking Jean Risker with it.

It rammed into the back wall, drawers popping out and crashing on either side of Dana's boss. The back of her chair hit, momentum whipping her skull into the wall with a thud and a crack like a mallet striking a croquet ball. The edge of the flat desktop jammed into her stomach.

The eyes – blue, lucid, cool, and shrewd thirty seconds earlier – bugged out of a white mask above her fractured nose. Then the marketing director erupted, vomiting blood out of her mouth and nostrils. It gushed and spattered on to the desk, over the powdery white heap that sat there like old business.

Dana was standing in the doorway.

"Yes?" Risker said.

Dana blinked.

"Is there anything else?" She was looking up from behind the long desk with the PC-compatible on one end and on the other, the gold-framed photograph of a man jogging down a short hill, proving that connubial bliss had not been overlooked in the life of the tin director with the wide gold necklace and perfectly styled hair.

"No. No, thank you," Dana said. She was feeling light-headed.

Risker swivelled twenty degrees in her chair and clicked a switch on her speaker phone. "John, the quote from Chiat/Day is on my desk . . ." Her voice asserted itself in John McCutcheon's office. His time was her time.

Dana turned in the doorway and headed back towards her cubicle. Beige and grey, coordinated to tranquillise, vibrated around her. Potted plants watched her like Risker's stooges.

Dana opened her eyes into the brightness. Then she clamped them shut again, tight as safes. She rubbed them, trying to clear the pictures behind the lids. She flipped over and took deep breaths. By the time she flipped over again, her heart was beginning to downshift. She wasn't shocked any more. She was just tired of the episodes, tired. What were those thoughts but leeches? She imagined singeing her memories of Jean Risker with tiny blue flames. They dropped off one by one.

She forced her thoughts backwards, away from her job to Louis at the table, away from the table. She was relaxing again in the warm sun. She was getting sleepy. The waitress in the Shutters with her blonde hair sprayed firmly into place seemed to billow in from a cloud, carrying plates of buckwheat pancakes and eggs. Her tag displayed her name and where she hailed from: "Rowena from Sparks".

Louis and Dana were walking after breakfast, down the main drag with no lights, only four-way stops. They entered a crosswalk, and a station wagon slowed and stopped six feet away instead of challenging them as cars did in the city.

Dana felt her belly. It was oily and warm. She dropped her arm back to her side, palm up, inside of her forearm to the sun. Sleepy. The women's store. Mannequins in dresses of no identifiable decade, fashionless, outside of time. Pastel greens and plaids and floral patterns. Deep hems. A square pocket on a long dress, yellow plaid on white. Mother.

Mama in the laundry room, slamming the lid of the washer down. Daddy beside her. She was talking loud, the way she talked on and on when she was mad. Her voice had that sound, tearing back and forth, back and forth on Daddy like a saw. His head was down and the light in the ceiling was bright.

The big bottles, plastic but heavy, full of stuff heavy as water but smelly, so strong it made your eyes water. Just out of reach. Her voice cut back and forth, deeper. Just out of reach until you get one and throw with all your might and see it hit her like a big fat cannonball in a cartoon and drive her out through the wall, and the wall crashing and breaking into rocks the size of the little rocks under the bushes outside. Reaching the bottles . . . reaching . . . until a hand slaps you down.

Dana squinted out over the bright water in the direction of the raft. A boy dived off the middle. A young couple sat on the left side and Louis on the right, staring off towards the shore, his legs dangling in the water.

She checked the man on her left. He was reading a magazine, lying on his side, facing in her direction. For the first time she noticed the line of dovetailing black hairs that bisected his belly from the solar plexus down. She could make out a photo of a weightlifter on one of the pages. Probably *Sports Illustrated*, she thought. Probably the swimsuit issue.

Bodies shiny with water were bobbing in and out close to the shore. Heads were slick wet caps of colour. A young girl took tentative steps in, walking gingerly on the stone bottom. To Dana's left, a pregnant woman and a man in knee-deep water were helping a small boy on to a rubber raft. His thick blond hair, nearly white, made his little bony torso look even tinier, birdlike. He flopped down and paddled gleefully on both sides of the raft. His mother, at least seven months gone, stood up and pressed her hands against her lower back.

Dana checked her watch. Not quite twelve thirty. A radio was playing behind her, and teenage girls were giggling and jabbering, the tones of their voices sweet and effervescent as diet pop. Dana recognised the song but didn't know what it was or who did it. Something about "give up on the illusion" or "live up to the confusion". It could have been both.

She closed her eyes again and let every bit of leftover tension drift out. In a few minutes the rest close to sleep was returning, like massage working deeply, down through the muscles, down to the consciousness. The image of Rowena in her pinkish uniform dress returned, the blonde waves and apron with wide pockets and the white name tag. The plates were gone and she held her two hands out. It was a kind of supplication, palms upwards.

Dana extended her hand and Rowena took it. The waitress smiled quietly and turned Dana's hand over. With the tip of one finger, she began tracing the lines in her palm. "Give up on the illusion," Rowena said, looking sweetly, so calmly, into Dana's eyes. "Give up on the illusion."

Rowena's grip on her hand, warm and firm, was much like Noah Taggart's. His way of shaking her hand deliberately was an assurance quietly repeating, asserting itself. Dana saw his eyes again that seemed to shift from brown to black, drawing colours from the room, drinking them in.

Soon Noah Taggart's eyes were like a great murky shadow settling down on her. She heard a sound, faint at first then louder, like a raspy intake of breath through a dry throat. It was difficult to breathe.

Taggart's stare was crowding her, and she could not turn away. Even in the dream, Dana knew that if she could only turn her head, she would be able to do it soon. But not soon enough. Taggart's stare was oppressive, paralysing, like thumbs on her eyelids, holding them closed.

His face was closing in like a huge pillow over her eyes

78

and nose. There was a screaming. It was somewhere in the sound of laboured breathing, in the dark centre of Noah Taggart's shadow that was inching in like choking pillows.

When the small, plaintive scream faded, Dana wanted it back. It was like a lifeline somehow, and her insides were sinking, drowning. When it came again, it was like a siren piercing a deep dream in the small hours of the night.

Her eyes were open. Two little girls ran by on the beach, racing, screaming with excitement, screams like sweet music. There was beach again, and blinding water, the white sand and the lake that was coming into focus deeper than blue. No bad dream. No sombre presence weighing down like an alien atmosphere. And – as Dana realised, wide-awake and with both eyes open – no Louis.

The same couple were sitting on the left end of the raft, arms around each other. No boys diving and no Louis. She told herself to keep calm. It was her mind again, running away. Fight it. Beat it down.

She searched the water, examining each swimmer. She could feel her heart begin to hammer. Maybe he was swimming underwater. He wouldn't with his glasses.

Dana sat bolt upright. She checked the beach to her right, searching the crowd. All of them were out for pure pleasure, vacation. That seemed suddenly horrible.

She glanced the other way down the beach. Where was he? Nothing had happened. It was the fantasy. Nothing had happened. He had not been choking, drowning out there under a heavy layer of water, clutching through a poisonous atmosphere as dense as smothering pillows.

Her eyes fell on the fat man. He had risen on his arm and was watching her, staring at her unabashedly, a mindless grin on his face. How could he look like that? Was he amused by her, seeing her so defenceless against the wild thing that was beating like a fist at her insides now, clutching in her gut?

Dana's eyes went black. Hands on her face blinding her, seizing from behind.

She screamed and thrashed her head and as she fought

her way to her feet, she hooked one foot on the chair, losing her balance and pitching on to her knees in the hot sand. Louis was standing stiffly behind the chair, looking as though he had stepped on a snake.

"No!" she was shouting hysterically. "No!"

People were turning. Louis knelt down and crawled over to her. He opened his arms.

"Jesus, I'm sorry," he was saying. "You okay?"

She nodded and they fell together and Dana held on, trying to stop the sobs she could feel were coming, but they came anyway.

When she caught her breath she told him it was okay, it wasn't his fault. She had a dream, that was all. He asked if she wanted to leave and she told him no. They went into the lake together and, as Dana smoothed the cooling water over her arms and shoulders and back along her temples, she imagined she was washing the creeps off her body and out of her head.

Before returning to Alpenhurst they lay in the sun to dry. Dana kept her eyes open on the bright afternoon, on the people enjoying the beach, even on the fat man who had seen Louis's little joke coming. By the time they left, they had both got plenty of sun and Dana had assured herself that she was feeling fine.

PART II
Noah Taggart

9

Dunn's Crest perched on the granite hill like an old weather-beaten bird of prey. Built in the nineties, the aged coats of paint on its frame walls were dirty brown, and the spots where it had cracked and peeled were scarcely noticeable, especially under the cold moon when its great standing shadow loomed on the rock among the huckleberry oaks.

It was a tough house. Everything that could fall from the two storeys and the gabled roof had fallen already. What remained persisted with a will as hard as granite from the old abandoned quarry a short distance down the hill. Only the shutters were loose, a minor concession to the elements, and they banged in high winds when the winter storms thundered up the Sierras.

From outside in the early evening the lights on the first floor made thin yellow cracks between the curtains. The light came from the old sconces on the walls in the long, narrow hallways. They had once burned gas.

Beside one, a tall man leaned on a long straight arm against the wall. He bent over the woman in front of him, talking quietly. The light softened her hair. She was smiling up at him as he spoke, dark eyes heavy with liner and mascara. She had a lazy, languorous way of standing in the light summer dress, weight shifted to one leg and hip slightly out. The man seemed to hover over her, drinking in her dusky perfume. If he had seen her standing alone in a clearing of wildflowers, fixing a purple phlox in her hair, he might have followed her anywhere.

Kenji Sukaro appeared, passed the couple without a word, and entered a large room farther down the hall. Only the dim light from the sconces in the hall fell into

83

that room. Music, primitive-sounding like a skin drum and a reed pipe, could be heard, but so faintly, it must have been coming from elsewhere, possibly down below, up through the time-worn floor and the ancient musty rugs.

Half a dozen men and women lingered in the room like shadows. A few were moving, nearly imperceptibly, to the music. Most wore dark clothing, even Kenji, whose black *haori* made his face seem pale, the colour of white ash.

To the left of the door, three figures slumped on an ancient horsehair divan. One stood as Kenji entered the room. He extended his hand and the two clasped forearms, exchanging nods but no words. The eyes, black and white, seemed to loom at Kenji out of the darkness. His face was shiny black and his tunic was grey muslin, and all of the black man seemed to absorb the light, reflecting nearly nothing. His eyes were exceptions, and a diamond pin that sparkled on one ear.

Kenji drew his other hand from a pocket, fist-closed. He held it out then opened it, palm up, revealing a tablet the size of a quarter. Thinner than a coin, a bit thicker than a communion wafer, the disc looked grey-green, like moss or lichens, mottled with tiny fibres.

The black man's gaze dropped to the tablet then returned to Kenji's eyes. He extended his hand also, turned it, opened it. A tablet of similar size and thickness lay red and shiny in his pink palm like a polished stone, bright as blood.

Their hands lay side by side, palms up, not touching but close enough for one to feel the other. The black man watched Kenji's face and waited. Kenji's gaze was narrow and unyielding, his face expressionless as Buddha.

From the corner, beneath one of the oil paintings that hung like dark squares against the smoky walls, a young woman in boots and hooded pullover was watching intently. Kenji saw her without looking. The woman knew, and she watched but did not come closer.

Kenji's hand turned. It slapped down on to the black man's palm, and he pushed up against the sudden weight. The pellets crushed between their hands. They ground their

84

palms together, breaking the pellets into powder, mixing the powders.

Finally, as he had begun it, Kenji relaxed the pressure. For another moment their hands lay together, and then Kenji's hand lifted and turned. The powders in their palms were the colours of vegetation and blood. The dark-haired woman in boots was coming closer.

With great care Kenji brushed every particle of dust from his palm into the black man's upturned palm. With a small silver spoon from his pocket, the black man began to stir the powders. Soon they were as fine as confectioner's sugar and thoroughly mixed. The woman stood between them, eyes hungry. Her lips twitched and she dragged the back of her hand across them. Kenji gazed into the powders, waiting. The music of the congas and reed pipe hovered around them.

The black man dipped the spoon into his palm and lifted it to Kenji's mouth. The woman's laugh sounded animal.

Kenji's lips closed around the spoon, and when he drew it out it was clean. The black man dipped the spoon again, taking half the powder that remained in his hand. No sooner had it disappeared in his mouth than the woman, giggling and whimpering, seized his open hand and ate from it greedily. Then she licked it like a dog, with long strokes of the tongue.

The black man laughed and held the back of her head as she licked his palm. Soon Kenji was laughing too and the woman, clenching the black man's wrist and hand, laughed, showing her coated tongue, then licked hungrily again, cleaning his skin of every bit of dust.

Seconds later she had finished and she wasn't laughing at all. The two men were beginning to move casually to the music. She stood between them, glancing from one to the other. The music was quick and simple, like heartbeats and the whistle of wind.

The woman knew that she would be relaxing soon, she must. She would be where the men were. But it wasn't soon enough. What if nothing happened this time?

When the other man appeared, stepping towards the

three of them from the shadowy corner where he had been watching, she wanted to hope but dared not to. The way Kenji and the black man looked – they made her afraid. It was as though they didn't see her or the tall man at all. They were moving to the pagan, hollow beat in that other place. They were already there.

Although she knew the man as well as she knew anyone in the room, it was difficult to be sure as she examined his boyish face, innocent as the moon. Was he really grinning at her? What did it mean? He answered by extending his right fist, turning it over, opening it.

She tried to show all of her gratitude in her smile, but how could she? She felt like hugging him as she took the tablet the colour of deer moss from his palm. Perhaps she would hug him soon. Their two hands lay side by side, nearly touching. The ruby tablet Lloyd Burris kept in his own upturned palm. Their eyes locked.

The music rose in the old walls like a pulse of the house itself. It settled from the shadows in the long halls. It even sounded faintly in the kitchen cupboards and haunted musty guest rooms, although those doors were closed and locked.

Noah Taggart heard the music all too clearly in his bedroom on the second floor. He dealt with it as he would an old, familiar pain. Actually, it was only an annoyance, so much milder than the knifing sound of electric music from a radio or the brakes or horns of cars.

Of course it was loud to him, much louder than to the others. He was accustomed to that. It was music of his own choosing, and if there was discomfort, there was also stimulation in it, the rhythm like the one that fired the blood, and the pure human tone of breath across the mouth of the pipe.

In the oval mirror above the dresser, he adjusted the tunic. All black and simply cut, nothing about it drew attention. It threw Taggart's face into relief, adding black to his eyes, deepening them, much the way faces, especially eyes, were showcased by tuxedos or mourning clothes. Such was not Taggart's intention.

86

In the mirror his hair, black and grey, swept back like smoke above his forehead. It interested him as little as the features of his own face. He was not inattentive to his appearance, however. He knew that to the others it was a condition of commerce, a set of understandings they shared. Of all qualities, they trusted it most, the property they could see and therefore seem to know.

That was how Taggart regarded the appearance of the physical shell. He could participate in commerce by going among them in his disguise. Of course it was tedious. Of course it was beneath him. It was necessary nonetheless.

The other details were aesthetic: fine points of pleasure and beauty as it served pleasure. His clothes were only incidentally pleasing to the eye. Their real beauty was texture, smooth fibres inviting to the touch and tailored perfectly – no synthetic material with tiny plastic lashes, no seams ineptly done which lay like crooked agony against the skin.

The furnishings reflected in the mirror around him were valued for the same reason. That they were costly was irrelevant. Money to Taggart was a relic, quaint as a prior generation's hit tune. The fine brocade curtains suspended from the canopy above the bed, the sheets of satin and the robe of dark-brown silk, the fur-lined slippers and the shoes of calfskin, the chairs with their upholstery like velvet as rich and soft to the touch as the velvet curtains that hung darkly to the floor beside the window – the value of these was their transparency, their ability to be, yet vanish: without intrusion.

Senses tuned to insects emerging with nightfall, outside the house and a hundred metres down the hill, to the perfumes and human smells that flooded, dense and suffocating, through a drawing room – these senses were enemies. Taggart's clothes, his bed sheets, all the textures which encountered his skin were what they were because they respected the senses. They allowed them to exist in peace. They shielded him from chaos.

How fine, the others may have thought, how charming, when they saw Taggart and his worldly things. He adjusted the shoulder of the simple black smock. The familiar aroma rose from it: dusky smoke, incense like sweet clay, seasoned with the giving of life, exhaling the rot of evergreens, cedars and yew.

He was not smiling in the mirror, but he was smiling inwardly. They had agreed to accept such silliness, to trust what they saw with their own two eyes. It was the fundamental agreement among them that allowed commerce to take place. They surrendered it so grudgingly, like infants being weaned. Taggart's eyes in the mirror looked old, like stones, but he was smiling inwardly. Things were so seldom what they seemed.

He turned from the mirror. As he did, his gaze fell on the hall beyond the open door. A man and a woman were embracing there.

He knew them both: Paul Decker, a writer from Agate Cove, and Jenny Bloom, a waitress in the café on North Lake Boulevard. He understood the slender young man with his adolescent leather jacket and boots, understood his motives and their nuances, his every need. It was not the same as saying that he felt what the man felt as Jenny pressed against him while they kissed and his hand went lower on her back. Taggart understood that tugging desire; he enclosed it. He had taken it into himself so long ago that he did not feel it. What he knew was memory of desire, vivid recollection of a paltry thing.

They lacked understanding of their needs, how weak their desire was, how tenuous their attachment. That would come with time. They might never know how much more was possible. Trapped as they were, locked in the flesh, they knew nothing. Taggart could see it in their bodies, the minute movements each made to accommodate the other so that they seemed to match perfectly, casually fitting, as though intended for each other, in the rounds of love. They lacked even an intuition of true desire. Taggart knew that desire all too well, the need to possess physically and spiritually, the agony and the fulfilment it could bring.

It was difficult to believe that they could ever enter into consuming passion; consuming for both master and slave. Even the thought of it beginning again, the hint of a possibility that it could begin again, stirred something unpleasant in Taggart, like wind from an unlatched window. For Jenny Bloom or Paul Decker, what was disturbing to Taggart would be devastating, uncontrollable, a compulsion strange and dreadful, like a wild dog scavenging through their insides, with a craving for all that flowed in their veins. But almost surely, it would never come to that. They would never know Taggart's brand of passion, just as they would never be tortured by the sound of steel stroking a whetstone or stand in a crowded room among the drums of all the human hearts, a sound like the padded paws of wolves rushing after living prey.

They would know distance, he was sure of that. They would move away from each other inexorably. It was simply to be expected. The distancing would come with their new way of being: a necessary streamlining.

Taggart saw them part for a moment then kiss again, one of her hands behind his neck, the other in his hair. The desires that bound them were like cobwebs. They would snap as the distance grew. Taggart watched them clinging to each other like drowning men clutching flotsam. He tolerated them, as he tolerated them all.

He crossed the deep carpet to the window. Was it truly beginning again? Had the question returned to pose itself again, testing for a clearer response, a fingertip probing closer to the wound?

Beside the bed, one small lamp burned dimly. Taggart switched it off and held the heavy curtain back. Blackbirds were racketing on the rim of the quarry. Could it be beginning again or was it only a phantom, a shadow cast by ones in other places, other times? A shriek pierced the woods at the base of the hill: a woodchuck or ground squirrel. A ferret took its throat.

If the desire began again, there could be trouble. The new woman could be difficult, he had felt it at once. Of course, she would be useless as clay to him without the tension he felt when he pressed her hand and read her eyes, a charge not unlike heat lightning building between ground and cloud.

89

Of course she was a shadow. Surely she had once taken another form, but as always, traces had been added and others stripped away, like a canvas reworked through centuries. What came of that was unpredictable, even for Taggart. But her special property, the charge that betrayed her so eloquently, that much he was sure of. He looked out through the glass, trying to clear her from his mind. He heard the blood scraping in his own veins.

She was there in memory, a form he would never be rid of. Mara was coming in from the garden, descending the winding stair, rising from the bed. It flooded back, his hand on the cool, moist ledge and, rushing up from the base of the wall, the scent of flagstones damp in the night air. The memory was of Mara and a brief time of peace.

It was Bastille Day, Taggart thought, and laughed quietly. Midsummer. He recalled the other Bastille Days and fixed on one, inevitably.

Her perfume came from behind him in the room. He stood with his hand on the broad stone ledge, looking out the leaded window on the flagstone courtyard, down the satin hill in darkness, where no birds sang.

"They're ready, Noah. It's time."

He recognised the voice behind him as he had recognised the footsteps in the hall. He appreciated the way she had sent the two pitiful young lovers downstairs. Still, he wished the voice were one he did not know and could not anticipate. He wanted her voice to be like new music, original in every measure, unfamiliar, lacking connotations, incapable of washing over him in paralysing waves of sadness. What she had said would be correct. It would be time. Taggart dropped the curtain and turned to Frieda Beckman waiting in the door.

"They're assembled in the drawing room," she said, and stepped towards him. The dress she wore was cut straight across the neck – black and plain like his tunic. She stood beside him and touched his sleeve. Like the others, she wore no jewellery or makeup, and in the dim light, age coiled heavily around her eyes.

"They've prepared themselves?" he asked.

"Yes."

He nodded wearily and crossed the room to the hall with Frieda Beckman at his side. He closed the bedroom door and they began to descend the stairs towards the indistinct, throaty sounds, no longer exactly voices. Taggart heard also their quick, rough breathing. They were ready.

By the time they reached the bottom of the stairs, he had pulled his mind back from it – the leaded castle window high above the Adriatic; Mara's scent in the ancient room; the new woman who, simply because she reminded him, could steal thoughts away so easily. The drawing-room doors were open. They were waiting inside: black figures in groups and pairs.

In the steps between the stairs and the door, Taggart gathered his attention in an instant, focused his thought like one pure tone. He saw the target clearly, the man standing in his apartment in the city many miles away. As he entered the room, Frieda Beckman left his side and stood among the others.

Their eyes all fastened on him, eyes dark-ringed and hungry. They shuffled forwards stealthily, instinctively, as beasts to their feeding. No lights softened the room behind them. They wore no jewellery, no costumery of pageant. No candles flickered in the lily hands of celebrants.

Taggart searched the faces. All of them – Kenji and Lloyd and the others – all of Noah's flock. Now they were beyond those first expectations, the silly ideas that some mumbo-jumbo liturgy was to come.

There was no talk. Quiet shuffling feet in the room. Bestial pawing. Hunched advances and retreats. Scented smoke like spice to the tongue. Reed and drum. Their foul breath, their fast hearts.

Taggart's ribcage belled. His diaphragm dropped like a man's fingers interlaced, supporting weight. The others in the room responded instinctively. The sound of all the inrushing breaths was soothing to him, like the suck of the sea.

A sound began in his throat. At first it was a dry rasping, but it soon changed to another sound, one that humans did not make. It was like the screech of a bird or of something not quite a bird. It was like a call that might have sounded in the rugged moraines before time was kept; the cry of a massive winged thing more reptile than bird. Part screech, part howl, it forced up out of the dry cage of Taggart's chest, filled with tiny cries. It rose and fell in his throat, drawing forwards and back like a saw on dry bones.

Kenji Sukaro's jaw fell, his own rough howl beginning. Lloyd Burris's growl began, his legs immobile as pillars, his head writhing on his shoulders. Frieda Beckman's cry was a shriek, and out of the black man's upturned mouth came a sound pure and full from the gut, as though some old god were blowing his body like a horn.

The old house on the granite hill resonated with the roaring like a huge bell. The call was going out to the one in the city. The bell was tolling for him.

Down the slope, a red fox jerked its nose from a hole in a rotting tree. Was the earth starting to tremble? In the guts of the fox, hunger battled fear. In the next instant it turned and darted into the brush, leaving only spattered saliva behind it on the leaves. Eyes of terror stared out from the hollow in the root, the tiny furry body hunched and buried in the hole.

10

"Aannh." The sound honked from Barry Hilton's hatchet-shaped nose as he pulled out his chair. It was a buzzer meaning *wrong* to the answer, *The first day of summer*. Barry sat down first.

"What then, is today, smart-ass?" Barry's wife Michelle asked. Her black hair caught the dining-room light. It wasn't exactly spiked, just combed stylishly up with a fistful of styling goo. She thought she was smiling, but it looked like a wince.

"Bastille Day," he shot back, pleased with himself. All trivia questions to which he knew the answers delighted him, especially his own.

"After Jacques Bastille, inventor of *le commode*." Brian Thomas was starting to peel the foil from the cork of a Domaine Chandon. With a flourish, he pulled out the chair opposite Barry for Michelle to sit.

"*Pas du tout*," Barry continued. "For the start of the French Revolution, we should have fireworks."

"Fireworks we've got!" Brian declared and popped the cork into the living room. Then he swung the bottle to Michelle's glass to catch the bubbles.

He wondered where the cork went. He saw it hit the top of the Levelor blinds, then he lost it, although he imagined hearing a little bop in the vicinity of the CD player. He knew it was a stupid thing to do, but his nose was numb and he was pleasantly buzzed. Besides, Michelle was smiling like she thought he was cute. Brian didn't much care.

He went on to Barry's glass, careful not to overfill. Brian wanted to eat. Rhonda appeared from the kitchen in her slinky white dress as though she had been reading his mind.

"Barry, could you help me?" She was aiming a silver serving plate at the centre of the table. Her fingers were all rings.

"Oooh," Michelle cooed. "Gorgeous."

Barry guided the plate down gingerly and regarded it with awe. It could have been the Maltese Falcon.

"Salmon mousse," he said. "Rhonda, you knew salmon mousse was my favourite." His smile was unnaturally wide. Barry was excited. The dining-room light reflected from his teeth and glasses and from the surface of the receding hairline that looked tense and shiny. "How did you know?"

"Devious ways," Rhonda said coyly and sat down. It was enough to make Barry shoot Michelle a bug-eyed wink, acknowledging that she had been the accomplice.

Brian knew it had nothing to do with Michelle, that he had suggested the mousse and picked out the salmon. Michelle looked at Rhonda innocently, pretending it was their little secret. Rhonda surveyed her work: the moulded pink creation on the scalloped tray; on the glass table the clear glass plates with red, white, and green deco triangles;

watercress and endive salad; asparagus with hollandaise; sourdough baguette; in the kitchen, the apricot tarts.

"It's so gorgeous," Michelle enthused, "we should say grace."

"Grace," Brian blasphemed and started to pull out his chair. Michelle began cackling inanely. Jesus, Brian thought. Barry grinned too but regarded the food greedily, waiting for Brian to serve.

Brian had indeed intended to sit. He had poured all the champagne and nestled the bottle in ice. He was ready to sit down and propose a toast to Barry's promotion, which was the occasion for their get-together, and more importantly, to the Beatles, whose *Abbey Road* CD was playing.

His hand was on the back of the chair as he glanced at the Japanese print of five cranes on the wall behind Rhonda's head. The birds' black and white bodies and long white necks stood flatly against a gold background. In the space of that glance, Brian could sense what was coming.

"Hey," he said instantly. "Excuse me, guys. I'll be back in a sec. Go ahead, start." As an afterthought, he picked up his champagne glass, trying to seem festive. No cause for alarm. He hoped to God he would make the bathroom.

Rhonda was beginning to slice, not even suspicious, as he rounded the table. By the time he reached the bathroom door, his hands were sweating and his head felt as though a lot of blood had dropped out of it. He closed the door softly, gripped the counter, and stared into the mirror. Why the fuck now? Because, that's why. You didn't choose when.

The row of makeup mirror bulbs glared. A black-and-white poster of Madonna, looking very silver-screen like Harlow or Marilyn, reflected from the side wall. All the rest, towels and tile, were black and white and lemon-yellow. Rhonda's choice, all of it, slapping him in the eyes. He waited and watched the mirror and started to sweat like a fugitive. He was waiting for confirmation.

He didn't wait long. When it came, it was like a wave of nausea. He knew he wouldn't puke. That would be far too easy. There was a full, sickening sweetness to it like blood and syrup he was smelling and tasting.

94

The taste and the bad stomach came with a sound. At first it was indistinct, like a faint cry of a trapped animal. Then it was sharper, high-pitched and painfully close, a sound that scraped on the nerves like a dentist's pick on a molar.

His face in the mirror slipped out of focus. It was whitening like a movie dissolve. Was he losing consciousness? The face came back like a slide of someone he vaguely recognised. Why the fuck now? It had to be sometime.

When the spell passed, he bent over and splashed his face. Then he dried off and combed his hair carefully, poured the champagne into the sink and washed the bouquet down. When he was ready, he turned the doorknob and killed the light.

Instead of returning to the table, he walked straight down the hall into the bedroom, leaving the door open. Barry was laughing. Brian picked up the receiver. He knew they wouldn't be able to hear the buttons, but he pressed number nine anyway, three times, three more, then four. He turned slightly, to face the door.

He concentrated on speaking loudly enough to be heard in lapses of conversation. He had planned the call before the dinner, in case. He hadn't memorised words, but he knew the form they would take. It was important to make the protests long enough, forceful but not so strident as to be unbelievable to his friends and loved one at the dining table twenty feet away and around the corner, in the other world.

"Hi, Buddy, what's the problem?" Barry was the first to spot his long face as he returned to the dining room.

"People, I'm sorry," Brian started. He hoped to God he would finish before the next wave came. "It's the Banzhoff deal in Tahoe. He needs me up there tonight. Hyper-critical. He's got Banzhoff and his old lady at the lodge, and he thinks they're ready to close. A thousand pardons, guys. I feel like shit, but my hands are tied."

"Mixed metaphor!" Barry almost gagged on his wit.

Brian grinned and patted him on the shoulder then moved on to Michelle with a big hug and a smooch.

95

"Poor boy," she cooed. "You take care." She had that pinched smile on again. Was it a fragment of asparagus in her teeth?

Rhonda had been passing the salad. She looked up at him blankly. Did she know?

"Sorry. I'll call," he whispered as he pecked her cheek then headed for the front door. She nodded, but her mouth was a tight, disgusted line. Too bad.

"Ciao," Barry blurted through salmon mousse, no pun intended. Brian raised his hand. He had made it. He was in the clear, until next time. He stepped out and closed the door behind him.

Nobody. The high-rise hallway was quiet, but as he neared the elevator, he could hear the cables grinding and straining behind the doors. He passed the elevator and kept going. He didn't know when it would come again and he didn't feel like putting on a freak show.

By the time he reached the door at the end of the hall, he could feel it beginning. He pushed the handle and entered the stairwell and, as he started down, the cool, earthen smell of the concrete billowed up, suffocating. The door banged shut above him and he clutched his ears with both hands. He stood that way on the stairs until the deep shaft stopped reverberating.

Brian started down again. Four more flights. He could hear mumbling in distant rooms. Food smells were slipping under the stairwell door; aromas he could never have detected if he had been himself. Only himself.

He bounded down stairs, two and three at a time. He missed the handrail at the bottom of a flight and braked with his forearm against the wall. It didn't exactly hurt. He was feeling stronger, and even though his field of vision was bright and wavering, and perceiving depth was giving him trouble, all the particulars were crisper, saturated with colour and vivid.

He passed magazines stacked on a landing. Bright covers. Human trash. What were they for? A black number one appeared on a door. He passed it. He couldn't be seen. He wanted the basement door to the parking lot.

The last flight was darker, but it ended in a bright splash: clothes heaped on a white washer – red and gold, blue and orange. A yellow plastic laundry basket pulsed on the floor. A drier cranked and the cloth tumbled in the round window in a livid cascade. All the colours, red-tinged, rolled in his head.

Over the rumble of the drier he heard voices, just beyond the door at the far end of the room. Between himself and the back door, three bicycles chained together. He wasn't thinking of the fire-code violation or of blocked egress. They were steel beasts, enemies. The door at the end of the room was opening.

Brian heaved against the bikes and they crashed back in the short hall. "For Emergency Use Only" was a red blur as he scrambled over them and hit the release bar on the door. No alarm.

He started across the parking lot, jogging easily. It was after eight, and the sun had slipped below the tops of the buildings, but the asphalt had stored heat like a battery all day, and the black petroleum smell welled up from it. Auto exhaust mixed with the asphalt and Brian choked on it. But he sucked in more air and kept going.

By the time he reached the car, he was feeling faint. He sat and turned the key and waited for the air conditioning to take over. A seagull screamed above the car. He closed his eyes. Soon it was cool inside the compartment. Brian took the wheel and, as he began to drive out of the lot, he knew he could make it all the way. But first there was a stop to make.

It was late, but he was betting the Fotomat would be open, and it was. He was feeling clear-headed and light and strong as he crossed the lot back to the grey Accord and opened the door. He pulled it shut and turned the key just enough to start the tape. Cool jazz floated from all corners – Paul Horn's flute and light percussion.

He lifted the flap on the envelope of photos and thumbed through the prints. He put back all but one.

The scissors were next, from the glove compartment.

Brian had snapped the shot himself. He recalled the occasion – a Saturday excursion to the Napa Valley with Louis and Dana. They were standing, arms around one another, Rhonda in the middle, the grey stone of the Christian Brothers' winery behind them. They had been dwarfed by the massive structure with its cool cellars, but you couldn't tell by looking at the photo. Brian had pulled in close, so the faces could be seen clearly. He had known what he wanted.

Something wasn't right. He reached for the volume control and raised it, just a touch. Better.

He began to cut slowly, one careful vertical line until two smiling heads dropped into his lap. Then he trimmed the other side, finally clipping the top and bottom, evening the rectangle.

He looked down at the face that remained, feeling excited, but at the same time, sad. Photos always had that strange effect on him, the way they seemed to cut the strings that bound your memories; snippets out of time.

He reached into his pocket, unfolded his wallet, and inserted Dana's picture carefully into it, between a laundry ticket and a business card, in the pocket behind the bills.

He crumpled the trimmings of the photo and opened the door a crack. He felt guilty, not about destroying their images but because he was littering. He closed the door. It couldn't be helped. He needed to get going.

He replaced the scissors in the glove compartment. Then he fastened the shoulder belt, turned the key until the engine caught, and rolled out of the lot, heading towards the interstate on-ramp and the long stretch of highway that lay ahead.

Twice he nearly lost consciousness on the road, but each time left him more pure. He was like fuel. He could keep going. He would give them what they wanted.

It was sometime after midnight when he arrived. He didn't recognise the dirt road as he pulled off on the shoulder. It was a side road like the next where he stopped in the dark guts of the woods. In the night air, green-tinged by the huge trees, he relieved himself at the bottom of the shoulder. As he climbed back to the car, the moon was coming down like a sickle. He cowered in the seat, sweating, hiding like prey. He was in their territory now.

In the long hours that followed, Brian had dreams. He was growing uncontrollably, weights on his bones, bending them, stretching his skin tight. He was standing naked, balanced on one foot, arms raised. Before him, the bulky shape loomed, massive, the house of shadows on a hulking promontory of rock, like a huge galleon without a helm, dead in the water.

In the house or behind it was a roaring sound. Brian tried to open his eyes. It was bearing down, targeting him, straight through the middle of the shadow. In a moment it was on him, and it popped his eyes open, a loud rushing suck of wind.

As he watched the semi's tail lights recede, finally dipping down the hill out of sight, he noticed another sound. At first he thought the steady pulse was his own heart, but as he listened it faded. The realisation felt icy but thrilling. He could lock on. He had brains from the Livermore Lab, guts from the Pentagon. He waited until he couldn't tell whether it was sound or the memory of sound that he heard — the heartbeat of the driver in the semi cab or a fading echo.

Brian felt cold in the bone. He checked his face in the rearview mirror. At least the stubble was familiar. It certainly was a new day, wasn't it? Who would know the difference up here? Something had happened to the eyes. The point was, who would know? Pearl-grey mist was beginning to lighten outside the car. It was time to get going.

He headed back to the main road and followed it towards town. He didn't have to know where he was going — they did. He pictured them all in that barn of a house in the room dank as a dungeon where he himself had stood. They knew and, through them, he would know soon. All too soon. They had him by the guts, pulling him along like a dragline.

He was trembling as he started down the sidewalk on the tree-lined street. The mist was lighter and the dew was on everything like bright sweat. Brian's hands were moist and cool. They seemed to him like machines.

Why didn't matter any more. Only when, and then when it would end. A sound started, piercing, scratching inside like a pick, like tiny claws at the base of the skull, in the chambers of the ear.

He was moving fast, half running, half walking. It was difficult to control his stride. He forced himself to walk. Controlling his hands was difficult too. Tension was tingling in them, and he clenched his fists and released, clenched and released.

Rhonda knew, he imagined. Of course, she didn't know why. She wouldn't know that until the time came, and then it would be like everything else. She would simply take it because she needed what she needed and so did he. Brian looked down. Wet spots darkened the front of his shirt. He sucked in saliva and swallowed. A taste like iron. Bright sidewalk.

Trees clicked by and houses turned away. Brian's heart was charging. He felt strong and swift. He could vault hedges, slip through their windows. The sound in his ears was like muffled crying.

At the end of the block, he came to a playground. The ball field was deserted, the swings empty. It was only as Brian allowed himself to be drawn in through the open gate that he detected the human smell. It came on the breeze that brushed the back of the apartment house on the right side of the yard. He heard sounds, a rhythmic scuffing like dancing shoes, and that steady rhythm he recognised. They came from around the corner, at the end of the apartment building wall.

Brian began to jog across the short grassy yard. It didn't matter when, they could have you anytime. What made no difference either, you would do it.

He was on the short walk that ran along the building. His hands were twitching, curling, and he couldn't stop them from jumping up to his biceps. The morning air was shimmering, and through it, the brick and mortar wall, the rough surface of the sidewalk, the contours of each pebble and the yellow-green lashes of grass, all were so sharply defined, painfully precise. Around the corner, a human smell came from an alcove and, together with the steady beat, a rhythmic slapping and scuffing sound he knew.

She had been counting to herself, and when he rounded the corner, she went on skipping, the red rope hooping through the air four or five times even after she saw him. Stopping too soon could be bad luck. It took that long for her to know in her way who was standing there.

As Brian looked down at her, blonde hair and blue dress and white shoes, standing so small in the concrete alcove behind the high, windowless wall, he did not feel self-loathing or revulsion. Blonde was not blonde. She was nobody's daughter in the middle of summer between first and second grades. She was duty, absolute and undeniable as a baby pushing to be born.

When she dropped her rope and ran, he could sense every step before she took it, the way a stalking animal feels its prey, knowing it so well that it takes it into itself, becomes the prey also.

Around the wall, into an alley. Screams in the alley, but his ears shut them down. The target running before him, so small. He knew her terror, could feel it, just as he could feel the tender throat skin.

He scarcely had to jog to overtake her. Behind a dumpster, hoping he would pass. Froth, coating his chin, spattering his chest. Hands curled, steel hooks. Little girl smell.

At the end of the dumpster, she was crouching, wedged into the corner. There was a scream somewhere. She was looking at his eyes.

Fifteen minutes later, twenty at most, a woman's voice was calling.

"Julia."

It had called anxiously from the front steps of the apartment building and now it was coming closer.

101

"Julia!" the woman was calling from the gate, and her voice travelled out across the playground like a school bell no children would hear, emptying into a summer without end.

11

Whit Norwood punched zero, then he punched nine. On the screen, a snake was crawling between a woman's breasts. He put the remote control down.

They were bare, all right, and there were nipples. They weren't real, though. PBS wasn't into it.

"It mattereth little," he mumbled, and his head dropped back against the top of the recliner. There wasn't much around to contradict him.

It was past midnight, and Ellie was long asleep upstairs. On the wall behind him in the den, lighted only by the TV, a deer head protruded, a yellow warning diamond suspended from one antler: "Caution – Elvis in Trunk". Beside the deer hung a classic fold-out from an early issue of *Playboy*, a signed Vargas. She wasn't talking, lips in a pout. Across the room a mannequin stood in naked polystyrene splendour, toy holsters and a pair of six guns low-slung below the waist joint, silver boxing gloves on both hands, rubber monster mask. Next to the mannequin was an empty easel, and above it hung two styrofoam dice the size of carburettors. Drawing pads were heaped beside the easel, and four more lay on a table beside Whit's chair.

It didn't matter that the breasts weren't real because it was animation. Whit would have watched anyway, that was seduction enough. He couldn't turn away, even if it made him nervous to watch, as he knew very well it would.

The snake slinked down and the breasts became wheels and rolled off-screen. Then the snake began to circle and twist.

"Lariat," Whit declared. Hardly had he spoken the word than the snake formed a lasso whirling in air, gradually metamorphosing into a cowboy in pink duds at the end of the rope.

"Ha!" he almost shouted and reached for the glass on the table beside his pads. He swirled it and drank to himself. Scotch had only started to melt down the rocks.

"Comic-book minds," he thought. He had always liked Alan Arkin's line in *Wait Until Dark*. "They had comic-book minds." These guys telegraphed their punches. You could spot their clichés a mile away. Well, not everyone could. It took a discerning eye and a sensibility whittled keen.

He took another drink. In fact, maybe no one else on earth had picked up on the lack of originality in that little transformation. How many on earth, some five billion? How many croaking? How many hitting the cradle? He thought, almost solemnly, that it could indeed be true.

God, look at the rendering, he thought. Two cowgirls were approaching from the horizon on blazing scooters. It looked like they were drawn with a sponge. Or maybe it was all computerised, and they used those electric sticks on little tablets. Anyway, there was a reason it was on late-night PBS.

Foul! Whit checked himself. PBS was all right. He admired PBS. He was a member, sent them a cheque during pledge break. Anything to get pledge break off the air! But he did support them, that was the main thing. He let his money do the talking.

What he meant was, it was not network quality. He would not be misinterpreted. He would not be quoted out of context.

But shit. Look at that stuff! How did they get money to do that today? What was the budget for this little diversion? A skinny million or so? That turned a pretty good trick back in the Disney days. Meaning what? He took a dilute sip.

Meaning, simply, that you got the work of human beings of talent and vision and unrelenting standards that pride in their craft demanded. It kept food on their tables, not coke up their noses.

103

A string version of "Daydream Believer" was the sound-track. Too bad, Whit thought. He had always liked that little tune.

So, he mused, who was the controlling consciousness behind this farce of fluff, anyway? Who was the child-star director? What did he or she look like? He traded the Scotch for the top pad and a pencil. The Monkees' version of the song started, and by the time Davey Jones was done, Whit was finished too. He regarded it thoughtfully for a moment. The caption was "Portrait of the Artist". It had the head of Madonna and the body of Gumby. That seemed right.

He picked up the remote control again and punched through the channels. Championship wrestling. A test pattern of coloured bars. A war movie: dive bombers versus battleship. It could have been Corregidor. He always watched World War II movies when he was by himself and he came on them by accident or discovered the listing in *TV Guide*. He wasn't particularly proud of it, but he liked them because they seemed like part of his life; years of his life he would otherwise want to forget. It had nothing to do with John Wayne in the cockpit. Fuck John Wayne, for that matter. And the horse he rode in on. Hollywood reality. Comic-book minds.

John Wayne's plane was smoking, but he could still bomb. He tilted towards the ship and went into a steep descent, guns blazing. The sound of the strafing was soothing to Whit's ears, and soon he was asleep in the chair.

Dana Ferrin was suddenly wide awake in the bedroom in Alpenhurst, and she didn't know why.

12

At first she thought she heard something. She lay staring at the open door. Beyond it was the hall and it led to the stairs. Dana waited and listened.

It wasn't Louis – he was in the bed beside her. The

form in the bed that she sensed more than saw certainly was Louis. Wasn't it?

Her head snapped to the side. The man-shaped bundle under the quilt was turned to the far wall. She recognised his hair. Dana breathed again, but quietly. She was waiting to hear it again but hoping not to.

She was aware suddenly of the enormity of the house. Distance was a tricky concept in the dark. The farthest closet could be close if she heard a rustling in it. The hall seemed huge as she waited, watching the stationary forms of shadows from the bed. Her heart was starting to normalise. Then there was a snap out there.

Her breath hung. Her chest was only beating, and her hands clutched the sheet. She stared at the shadows in the hall, waiting for one to move.

Should she wake him? Don't be hysterical. Or histrionic – wasn't that what they called it now? You can handle it. It was probably just the house settling. The place was so huge, immeasurable, in the dark.

Eventually, she knew, she would have to look. Seconds passed. Longer than seconds. A minute. Maybe two.

Dana turned the quilt back and got up carefully. She didn't want to wake him if she didn't have to. She never slept in a nightgown, but her robe was on the back of the chair a step away, and she pulled it on. He was still sleeping. No other sounds.

The rug felt cool on her feet as she stepped towards the open door. When her fingers touched the frame, she stopped and listened again. It was quiet on the other side of the wall. She took the last step.

From the doorway, the hall was long and obscure at the far end, but there was enough light to see that it was empty. The small table opposite the stairwell, the pictures on the walls, were as they had been. The door to the second bedroom was open, as were the doors to the two guest rooms at the end, just as they always were.

She turned her attention to the stairs in the middle of the hall, the part she could see, nearly as far as the landing. She listened to it, and to downstairs. Quiet. She listened until the quiet itself seemed substantial, and a little scary.

That was it. The old house was settling, that was all. No threat, no sweat. As usual. It was funny what the mind could do. She flashed on the beach, how ridiculous she had been. She didn't make life easy for Louis, that was for sure. She wasn't proud of the fact.

But she could beat it. Someday she would get there – a nervous system as smooth as a figure skater, as even as a hand held flat, unwavering, at arm's length. Maybe partial lobotomy, she thought – a little snip snip. The way people get tummy tucks. Lobotomy. She had always thought it was a funny word. It sounded like a procedure to drop your rear end. But where would you drop it? Mid-thighs? Behind your knees?

Something moved behind her.

Dana jumped back against the door frame. Just to hold something. Just to get a hand on solid wood, on the bones of the house. Fortunately, she didn't shout. Louis was turning in the bed and the four-poster had squeaked.

She gulped a breath, then another. It was all nonsense, a squeaky old house. Or maybe a dream had wakened her. Louis's turning in bed, the firm sound of his body, was like a comforting voice calling her back in. You've done your duty. You can go back now. Dana checked the hall once more, just because it couldn't hurt, and went back into the bedroom.

Instead of returning to bed, she tiptoed to the bathroom, closed the door quietly, and turned on the light. When her eyes adjusted, she looked in the upper corner of the medicine cabinet where she had put the small brown bottle, label towards the back.

There really wasn't any reason to hide it; she and Louis had discussed whether or not she would take them on the trip. It was okay with him; she should have them if she needed them. Only if she needed them, though, they both agreed. Dana popped the cap and looked inside at the white pills like tiny flying saucers.

Halcion, Dr Rome's choice. Dana tried to remember

what Valium was like. That was Madelyn Pinsky's choice for nerves, after Placidyl for sleep. Dana had had Placidyl first, and she hated to think how long ago that was. Ten years? The dream had started it.

She was living alone then and working for a PR firm and in the middle of the endless break-up with Stan Morrill, the architect. Dana tried not to think of the dream. It could keep her up again. She looked in the mirror and tried to forget it, but her own dark brown eyes reminded her of the others.

It was a hospital with big transparent plastic bags full of trash in the corners of the halls, a county hospital. Only one nurse sat at the desk on the floor where her mother's room was. The nurse pointed and Dana followed the line of her arm. She could see only one door in the long hall. It was halfway open and she went in. A curtain concealed the bed. She put her hand on it. She pulled it back.

Beneath the sheet, the knees of the lifeless form were drawn up, twisted to the side. The body looked shrivelled, the birdlike chest nearly collapsed. The hands curled like small paws frozen in flight. But it was her mother's face that Dana always remembered most, the image that hit like a fist to the heart.

It was yellow-white, the colour of rags torn from a very old sheet. Her lips were bluish, and they made a taut oval, stretched to one side and fixed in place, a twisted form of the mouth in the painting that howled. They were Claudia's dark eyes, but diluted, paled with death's milk. They rolled up, away from Dana, not towards the heaven of our blessed Mother Mary, but towards the blank wall behind the steel bedstead.

Dana shook her head and tried deep breaths, counting the exhalations. It was a relaxation technique she had read in books more times than she wanted to remember. Would she need sleeping pills if not for her mother? They seemed to go together. Ham and eggs. Mom and drugs to beat the brain.

She was glad her mother wasn't dead, she really was. Death in the county hospital was not real, would not be real. The image in the dream, every single stroke that

107

painted it, had been put there by Dana over time, over years – many years, in fact, as she had understood from each of four therapists. How much had all that cost in money and grief and lost time? Better not think about that. Would she ever have seen one if not for Mom? Did she really only go to therapy because she knew one day she would have to see her mother's dead face and go on living?

All the kids would have to face her death one day. When Joe went, it was terrible and they all grieved. For Dana's brothers, it would probably be the same when Claudia died. Not the same exactly, but simple in the same way. For Dana it would be different. The death of one mother became different deaths to all the kids.

Kids. That was another matter. Dana couldn't want them. If it turned out this way with her child, she couldn't stand it. Things had been okay between her and her mother once, they must have been. There was a sometime she had confidence in, although she couldn't quite remember it.

She looked in the mirror again and the eyes were just her eyes. She had not done so badly with her life, even though it felt stuck together with transparent tape at times. If she asked herself how she felt deep down, whether Louis and she would always be together, she couldn't answer yes. That was no surprise. She couldn't imagine feeling that about anyone who seemed to love her. What she felt for Louis was as solid as she could feel for anyone; she could honestly say that. In fact, she didn't know what she would ever do without him. That meant something, didn't it? It meant a lot.

She hadn't done poorly in the other area either: good income and good positioning for the future. Still, if it came down to it for some reason, she wouldn't mind living on nothing again, if they were doing it together. The money was actually pretty unimportant. It often seemed more important to him, and she could understand why.

She looked back down into the brown cylinder. Take one if you need it, it's what they're for. Agreed, she said to the voice inside, then snapped the white cap back on. She closed the medicine cabinet quietly and was careful to turn off the light before opening the bathroom door.

Even with her robe on, the room felt cool. When she took it off, she hurried to slip back under the quilt without squeaking the bed. Louis was on his back. As she pulled the covers up, he mumbled something and rolled on to his side again, back towards her. Had he been awake all the time, knowing where she was, wondering if she had taken a pill?

She thought of waking him to say she hadn't but decided not to. She could hear his breathing, slow and deep. She knew he didn't really disapprove; he wanted what was best for her. That made Dana feel good, and she reminded herself of it whenever that old snapshot of her mother's eyes threatened to return. She reminded herself several times over the hours as she lay with eyes open and listened to every snap and tick of the sleeping house.

13

Tock.

Tick tock lock pock.

Tock.

Tock. Tongue click on roof of mouth. Tock.

The rhythm was steady, like a pendulum swing in the grandfather clock of the tall trees.

Tock.

Tick tock lock pock.

The trail twisted up a short hill and seemed to disappear for a moment in a clump of Sitka spruce. She nosed into the brush at the bottom like a porcupine and kept going. The hands of the berry bushes never scratched, just patted her along.

Tock. Tock.

Go away. Snake. Rat face. Go away.

Hands can grab the root, pull up. In the clear.

She made it to the other side of the brush and rose to her feet in the small opening. Sunlight was funnelling down.

Stump. Rock. China. Three four seven eight.

Across the brief clearing, she hopped for a moment on to the stump, wide and flat and scored by hatchet blades, and jumped down nimbly. The roots were high but her foot hit at the angle it had learned well, and she kept going across the pine needles.

She went on to the boulder, cool round surface, then giggled and ran towards the base of the big oak. It was a favourite because of the hole. Bored in its base, it was black inside, and even if you stuck your arm in, there was still more than you could reach. It could go to China. Cool and spongy in there. Green and black under the fingernails when you pulled out.

Tock.

Muddy bark. Bloody bark. Five six nine ten.

She crossed the fallen log that ended nose-down in the mud. Then on to the tallest tree she knew. As she always did, she tagged it with her hand on the heavy corrugated bark with the distinctive russet-orange colour inside, the blood colour of the Ponderosa pine.

Past the big tree, she crouched down and crept in through bushes that would have looked impenetrable to the ordinary traveller. She picked her well-worn way among the roots, and the branches and foliage made a ceiling inches above her head.

A bird flushed from the bushes and flew out over a grassy clearing, then ducked into the tree line on the far side. In a moment she crawled out of the bushes through a little opening the size of a dog door and stood up on the edge of the same clearing.

Fly around. Swoop down. Yellow cap. Blue cap. You could stoop and swoop, keeping low. Just brush the yellow tops and the blue tops.

In the grassy opening, goldenrod and phlox bloomed yellow and light purple. She made her way across like a stunt plane, arms out, twisting and swooping, coming in low to buzz, wing tips just grazing the flowers. Now and then a bee flew up, but it didn't sting. It flew so hard, it disappeared into the sky. Tumble bee. Humble bee.

She turned sideways to slip in between the bushes on the

110

far perimeter of the grass. The carpet of leaves and needles felt spongy and still moist in spots even though the sun had been high for hours.

In front of her the light lay in bright patches on the leaves. It was like a magic land, the cool shade down below and the tall straight trunks of the fir trees like foot soldiers of a fairy queen. They talked to one another, but so slowly a single word took weeks. You had to listen carefully, and she did, going from trunk to trunk, standing on the roots when they spread out from the trunks above ground, like the points of irregular stars. She put her ear to each trunk and listened. It was there inside, kind of a hum. They were talking from inside.

She hopped up, then down, then up again on a length of root that grew in the middle of nowhere, like a thick rope bowing up from the ground. It was another favourite place, not just because of the talking trees and the bouncy root, but because of the little patch which she knew lay just ahead. She hadn't been there in a while, but she remembered the sun, even on the days of the longer shadows. It always seemed to be shining in there, warming the bed of thick grass, where she could lie down and sleep or turn over and watch the birds hop on the branches and dart between trees.

Once again, she knew exactly where to push into the bushes, missing the poison prickles. Go around the bush with the webbing, the kind the worms liked to make. Slip by the next one then under the last. There it was!

The pool of grass looked warm and light as goose-down. She got up and skipped in, and the thick grass pulled against her shoes.

Plane again. Arms out, whirling in the grass, looking up and turning and the big wheel of treetops rotating around and around the ring of sky. Flop down soon, back in the soft grass. Turn and turn and when you're dizzy –

It hit the back of her leg and she tripped. It felt like a big root, but in the instant that she fell backwards into the grass, she remembered no root there, and if someone had put a root or something else in the sunny clearing, who had done it? There was buzzing around her, much buzzing going all around and up over her head. The back of her leg lay across the obstruction when she sat up to look.

No! She jerked her leg back, knee tight against her chest. No no! Go AWAY!

The body in the grass reminded her of something. It lay on its back, and although the back was arched, the stomach did not protrude. In fact, there was little stomach left. The irregular cavity in the shirt front had been pecked and clawed to shreds of black stain.

The head lay to one side, and it would have been staring directly at her if the eyes had not been pecked into empty sockets with a few fibres dangling inside like the stringy pulp of a jack-o'-lantern. The throat was a ragged gash in flesh that resembled sunbaked rubber, and the skin on the forehead and temples had dried nearly black and pulled taut against the bone.

The man's lower jaw hung like a door off its hinge, one side sprung open, matted with old black blood, the same substance that caked what remained of the shirt beneath the throat and still lay like spilled paint on the grass around the head and shoulders. The baked-on blood spattered even his pants leg, the outstretched leg that had felt too big to be a root.

The buzzing that had gone up was coming back down. The flies that had billowed up from the carcass when she tripped were settling back to their work, swarms of house flies and fat black and blue ones that looked iridescent in the sun. The body reminded her of something.

Flies landed and scurried in the open remains of the guts. Like tiny spaceships, they cruised in under the side of the open jaw.

Daddy came back – Go away! Go AWAY!

She scrambled backwards like a crab through the grass then flipped over, up on knees, up on feet and running. The bushes around the clearing had become a wall with no doors. There were no more ways in or under.

No! she screamed and tore in, ripping at the leaves. Branches snapped back in her face and prickles whipped against her as she pulled through. Then she was in the trees, dashing through the trees that were talking. About her. About it too. The trees knew.

She reached the clearing of flowers and ran out into the centre. Suddenly she stopped.

The trees had told her. The trees knew all about it and they told. It was not Daddy. That was a long time ago. She was there on the hot pavement with the car wheel that kept spinning in the air and the red lights that went round and round and Mama too. That was too long ago.

Then they went up somewhere. That's what Denise said. She couldn't tell Denise. Whenever you found something, you couldn't tell anybody. They just got mad and said don't go in the woods. Don't go in there.

She wondered what the flies were doing. She wondered how long it would take for him to be just like dirt.

She walked back in among the talking trees and picked the familiar way into the bushes, wedging in, then under. She went to the other side of the body, the one she hadn't seen. Then she squatted down just close enough to hear the buzzing.

She felt a lot better. It was not Daddy and she didn't have to tell anyone. It was one more thing she knew about, and she knew about a lot of things. Nobody thought so, but she did. She would just watch for a while.

If you tapped the blackened forehead with your finger-nail, was it all empty inside? Would flies come out? What would it sound like? Tock. Tongue on the roof of the empty mouth. The sound of something in a hole. Tock. She would just watch for a while, and listen.

14

Dana felt like saying she was sorry but decided she shouldn't. There was no reason to emphasise the negative, even though either of them would have trouble finding anything good to say about it. Instead they hugged and kissed one more time and Louis got in the car and pulled the door shut. He was looking down. She bent over into the window.

"Hey, they can't keep you more than a day," she assured him. "Tell them I said so. We'll do something fun when you get back."

"Probably two days at most. Be careful, okay?"

Louis didn't know exactly what he had in mind. Maybe it was just that he pictured her all alone for a couple of nights in the big house, or maybe he was thinking of the Chevy Nova they had rented the day before when he had phoned in and heard the nauseating news that, yes, they needed him in the office for a while. It was in good shape, though, an '87. There wouldn't be any problem.

"You be careful. Call me when you get there."

She kissed him and stood back and the car rolled the first few feet of the four-hour drive to San Francisco. She'd be okay. It was the deal he had agreed to for a little more time. So had she. Louis was suddenly glad they had gone to the party. At least she would have some names to call, just in case. He still didn't want to leave her. He always wanted to be close enough to protect her, whether it was really necessary or not.

Dana was still waving when it disappeared into the trees. She was a little dizzy. Louis's leaving felt like a sudden vacuum in the yard. Also, she had left her glasses inside, and the sunlight was really too much. It seemed to reverberate from everything, the driveway stones and the shimmering grass. She hadn't been sleeping well for the last couple of nights – no nightmares, just sporadic waking that was keeping her from feeling rested – and it made the brightness hard to take.

She turned and went back in and decided to do exactly what she had planned earlier. She was missing him instantly, as she knew she would, so the best thing would be to get out of the house.

Every morning they drove down to the lake for a swim and sun, and she decided to stick to routine because it was comforting. She didn't want to think much about the fact that the first week of their vacation was behind them, and now she had no choice about Louis leaving her alone. He had made his deal, and they probably would get most of another week out of it. There was no guarantee, though. What if they kept him the rest of the week? Deep down, she wanted him to tell them where to get off, but he wasn't exactly in a position to do that.

Just to have sound, she kept the TV in the bedroom on as she changed into her swimsuit and beach clothes, white drawstring pants and yellow smock. If they do keep him, she thought, she would just go back to the city early. She should be able to drop off the car there, that seemed reasonable. It seemed reasonable but probably wasn't. What were the odds that High Lakes Rent-a-Car of King's Beach had a drop-off return service? Practically nil.

She could take a bus back. Great. Dana didn't even want to think about that, but she could do it if he couldn't get away.

As she carried her beach bag downstairs, she could feel herself getting tense. She went into the kitchen and put her usual Diet Seven-Up, apple, and bran muffin into the straw bag.

It would be okay. He might be back in a day. Might. He had said two days. Who knows what that would turn into? She slammed the refrigerator door without really meaning to. It popped open and she pressed it closed gently.

As Dana headed for the front door and took out her keys, she was talking out loud.

"Okay, settle down. He'll be back. Relax."

She locked the door behind her, got into the little olive Chevrolet, and found a station she could turn up loud.

As she rolled out of the drive and left on to Tallac, she admitted she was feeling pretty lousy. Not enough sleep? Probably. She had that familiar tired-in-the-chest feeling. She didn't think she was sleeping that poorly, but maybe she was having dreams and not remembering. Whatever it was, it made her mad. Take it easy, you can sleep in the sun. Just relax.

Dana rolled along Tallac Lane through the alternating

light and dark zones made by the tall trees. The radio was playing oldies.

"We gotta get outa this place," Eric Burdon howled, "if it's the last thing we ever do."

So what if it turned out to be the time of their lives. It might just be, given the fact that they were both closing in on the big four-o, and retirement didn't look exactly imminent. What were the odds that they would ever do Europe for a month or turn up a free timeshare in Ixtapa? Dana's hands twisted forwards and back on the steering wheel.

"Girl, there's a better life for me and you."

The narrow road was beginning to wind. On a curve, the inside wheels of the Nova just touched the shoulder, churning gravel and dirt. Dana let up on the gas and pulled back in lane.

So what if the goddamn brokerage cut their time in half. She had a few suggestions for them. Could they get by on her salary alone if Louis told them to fuck off? If so, for how long? Would they want to try? She was biting her lip. Was it worth it? What if – ?

A horn blared behind her. It was a low black car in the rearview mirror, close enough that she could see the driver's sunglasses through the tinted windshield. It blared again.

Dana realised she had been distracted. She had probably been going too slowly after skimming the shoulder, too slowly for locals who knew the winding road downhill, for local maniac assholes anyway.

She hit the gas but it was too late. The car gunned and started to pass, even though the line was solid yellow between the two narrow lanes. The only other car she had seen that morning, a station wagon, was coming slowly uphill, and they were both closing on it. Too fast.

The black car was a blur on her left. Accelerating to get out of his way had been a mistake. She let up, and her foot was just moving to the brake when the black car cut in. She had to hit it then, harder than she wanted to.

The brakes caught, fortunately. Unfortunately, the right side grabbed and the little car started to skid. She was sliding towards the shoulder that dropped off into a ditch, and beyond, a slope of rocks and dense trees.

The brake lights of the black car flashed, red rectangles. An irrational reflex caused Dana to pull back on the steering wheel. Her mouth was open but nothing was coming out. The front wheels of the Nova hit the shoulder. The station wagon whooshed by in the opposite direction, just missing the Nova's skidding rear end.

When Dana's car stopped, rear tyres still on the road and front end on the shoulder, the air filled with yellow dust and the reek of rubber. The engine died.

She looked up at the black car, rolling slowly, sixty feet ahead. Her heart was firing like pistons and her mouth was dry. She rammed the heel of her hand down on the horn.

From the driver's window of the black Toyota Supra, an arm rose. From the hand at the end of the arm, a middle finger stood straight up. The arm lingered in the air, taunting her. Do something about it, it said. He knew the driver was a woman, and Dana knew he knew.

The brake lights were red flags. Dana's stomach knotted and something clamped her temples like a vice. The horn was piercing, but she held it down, held it down. Finally she let up.

She watched the Supra for a moment. Would he back up? Would her car start again?

The arm retracted into the window slowly, deliberately, like a chunk of robot. Then the brake lights went off. It began to roll. It was rolling forwards. Would he turn? It lurched forwards, screeching on the blacktop.

Dana watched for a blink. The shiny low-slung car came apart on the road. The steel road shark had swallowed a bomb that went off in its guts. Windows blew out in crystal sprays. Doors flung open on both sides like wings, but it was only when the hood and trunk popped up, bouncing lamely on their hinges, that the fire started.

Orange flames gushed from the hood, then the trunk. When they met in the passenger compartment, the rest went up, blasting up and outwards chunks of seat and floor mats and door handles and smoky arcs of recently

117

human debris, dynamited comets of intestine and rectum, tongue and breastbone and penis and eye.

Dana sat and blinked, still racing inside, as the tail lights of the black Toyota coasted down Tallac Lane, dipping down the hill and out of sight in the general direction of the lake.

She would deal with the experience. The fact that she had a million times before actually gave her an edge. She would work on it with her therapist first thing when they returned. She would take deep breaths and settle down. Settle down.

She had to get off the shoulder. She pumped the gas and turned the key but the engine just cranked. Don't flood it. She turned the key and held it without pumping. Three, four. It caught.

She backed up and started shakily down the hill again. She could feel one armpit drip, and it was already in the seventies, but her hands and feet were cold and clammy.

She and her therapist would discuss the hallucination, Dana told herself, even though she knew the therapists didn't really understand it, none of them had. To them it was the issue of power and control. They would discuss what the fantasy might have been expressing and what was happening to feelings Dana couldn't show. Something about that approach seemed off the mark. All she wanted to do was make it real.

15

"How can you stand to drink that at this hour, Daniel?"

Frieda Beckman did not have to sound like a therapist all the time. In fact, she was sounding like a nag, and she knew it. It was one of the things she liked about Danny, the fact that she could drop the mask and even be bitchy, and that Danny could appreciate it perfectly.

"It's heaven on earth," he said, padding back from the

refrigerator in yellow flip-flops. "I'd say mother's milk, but she had rum in her boobs. It explains so much."

He sat back down at the table and took a sip from the glass of clear, cold aquavit. Then he smacked his lips. Watching him, Frieda was glad she had had breakfast hours earlier. When he crossed his legs, Danny's knee-length red satin robe fell open. He flipped one of the panels back demurely on to his knee.

"Do you think it's clouding up? I wanted to get sun today," he added, a little worried. "I'm picking up Carl at eleven. You're welcome to come if you want."

Frieda got up and went to the kitchen window for a north-west view up the hill. A few seconds earlier, as Danny was closing the refrigerator door, Dana had been in the midst of her close call on Tallac, less than two hundred yards above the house. Frieda saw clouds above the trees, but they were cumulus, tall and cotton-white.

Maybe she should go with them. They did enjoy her company, and she lent a kind of status to their outings. Danny did something of the same for her. In addition to filling one of the four bedrooms besides Frieda's own, and acting as houseboy and chauffeur, he made a quite respectable escort. He looked good in public; he had excellent bones. Aside from that, he could turn the masculinity on whenever he wanted, and he did without rancour when he accompanied her. He thought of it as a social skill.

"No clouds to speak of," she said. "You should have plenty of sun. I think I feel like staying here, though."

Danny watched her back as she looked out the window. He took another sip of the clear liquorice.

"What's chewin' on you, anyway?" He exaggerated his New Orleans accent. She was silent a moment.

"It's Noah," she said. "Something's wrong." Danny didn't like that tone. Worry in Frieda's voice was definitely upsetting.

"Why do you think that?"

"He's depressed. Probably acute, it's difficult to say. I haven't seen the tendency in him before."

119

"Is he in good health, physically, I mean? Maybe he has some problem – "

"Yes, perhaps."

Frieda knew it wasn't physical infirmity. That wasn't an issue. She knew what was. She knew very well.

"Maybe it's your imagination."

She turned to face him.

"No."

"It just could be, you know. You know what I think? I think you're down about something yourself. You haven't been quite with it for about a week. I can tell. You're just imagining it's Noah; he's really perfectly fine." Then Danny caught himself. "Whoa, girl. See, I like to play therapist too. But it's much too analytical for me."

He got up, crossed to the sink beside her, and ran water in his glass. Then he squeezed her shoulders and gave her a peck on the cheek. She could smell the odd anise aroma on his breath.

"Come on with us. It'll cheer you up. We can go to Ricardi's after. Prosciutto and melon, *tu souviens*?"

"Not today. You go and have fun. I have reading I want to do." She was thinking of research and notes for her book on the differentiated unconscious, which had been adrift in the sprawling third chapter for more than a month.

"Oh, all right, but you can think it over while I'm changing." Danny left her in the kitchen. "You'll have one more chance when I come down," he called, and then she heard his flip-flops on the stairs. In a moment, music went on in his room.

She could not afford to be so dependent. Noah's shadow elements were too powerful. Frieda knew all about him. She remembered the day they met at the Jung Institute in San Francisco, a weekend seminar. She could sense his integration, the way the elements of his psyche aligned, supporting the self the way steel bars reinforced concrete.

She realised that what she had noticed then was only a hint of Noah Taggart. Now she knew what he was capable of as well as anyone, far better than most. Because she did,

120

Frieda did not look forward to broaching the subject. But she doubted there could be any other way.

What did that girl know about him? Only a delusion. That was less than nothing. Attraction she could understand, but Noah was beyond that. As Frieda knew only too well, obsession was not rational when it chose its targets. The alliance with the girl was never meant for him. Everyone in the group knew that. It would be painful, possibly ruinous. The time had come to confront him.

Frieda looked at the print of the wounded buffalo on the wall, a detail from the Lascaux paintings. She would need to draw on all her experience and skill. She would choose the words carefully, and the time.

16

"Hi, it's me. Guess what?"

Dana was fumbling with the towel, trying to dry off with one hand, surprised to hear Louis on the phone again. He had called after work the day before, and they had agreed the next call would be after dinner, around eight. She was in her morning shower when she heard the phone ring.

"What?"

"I'll see you tomorrow around noon." He was talking softly, obviously calling from his desk. "They only needed me for two days, and they wouldn't have needed that if Harris had been here. He's been out schmoozing with bankers this week. Anyway, good news, huh?"

"Yeah, great news. Great!" She was a little slow on the uptake and she knew it, groggy from the night before. After lying awake for hours, she had taken a pill. She hoped Louis couldn't tell.

"I can't wait to see you," she picked it up. "How would you like to do something fun – maybe go to the South Shore? But you'll be tired from the drive – "

"No, that's perfect. I'll take a nap and we can go tomorrow

evening. Look up a place you'd like to go for dinner down there. You okay?"

"Sure, I'm okay. It's just been weird sleeping without you, that's all." She knew he knew what that meant. "But I'm sure I'll do better tonight."

"Okay," he said, "but listen. Why don't you call up one of the locals and see if they want to do something? Ellie Norwood, or Kenji maybe."

Dana told him she'd think about it, and then he had to get off the line. She was glad his tour of duty was over and glad she had heard the phone ring while she was in the shower but, as she padded back to the bathroom, she had to admit to herself that she was not feeling great.

It was still bugging her, screeching back into her head at random moments. She smelled burned rubber. The black Supra, halting in the road, exploding into a fireball and pelting down in smoking bits replayed in her brain again and again. She had been too keyed up to relax at the beach, even lying in the sun, and had driven back after half an hour and cleaned the house furiously.

Sleep had been bad that night. She had dreamed about it, and in the dream, the man's arm out the window was the first to go, poofing into flame like a torch. She lurched awake and tried to read, but only went back to sleep in the early hours with the lights on in the bathroom and hall and the TV snowing static.

The next day, instead of going to the lake, she took a long, solitary walk, hoping to clear her head. She also wanted to tire herself out so she would sleep that night. Sometimes that worked, sometimes not. That time it did not, and the pill had been the last resort.

The next morning the incident resurfaced as she was having granola in the breakfast nook, but hazily, blurring a little with time. It had been the same with Jean Risker and the little unpleasantness in her office. It had been the same all the other times. When they happened, they stuck around for a while then gradually fuzzed out, greyed into ghosts. Until next time.

Dana flipped through the weekly *Bay View*. Maybe it

wouldn't be such a bad idea to see somebody, she thought. Too much rattling around in your own brain was unhealthy for anybody, even normal people. Whoever they were.

Her eye went to an ad for the Sattler Gallery in King's Beach. Acrylics and oils by Terry Aldahl. The opening had been the night before. Neither the gallery nor the artist sounded familiar, but the idea of going with company was appealing. At least it could get her out of her own thoughts.

She went upstairs to get her purse and thumbed through her address book to "N". She had exchanged numbers with Ellie at Kenji's party.

She felt a little nervous about making the overture, but Ellie was delighted that she called. She had even tried to phone Dana once when she was out, and it was nice to hear that. It was also strange to realise that she was living in the country, where telephone calls were placed and went unanswered by machine. Ellie knew where the gallery was and volunteered the transportation. In an hour the Norwood Mustang was pulling up at the front door.

Ellie wore a white scarf with gold horseshoes up over her hair as they drove with both windows down. Her sunglasses, in combination with the scarf, reminded Dana of Ava Gardner. After they had been under way for a while, Ellie asked about Louis, and Dana confessed he had been away on business.

"Oh dear, I had no idea. How've you been making out in that old house? I hope you haven't been scared. You come stay with us; we have a guest room and we'd love to have you. Whit would too – "

"Thanks, Ellie, but I'll be fine. He's coming back early tomorrow."

"Well, I'm glad to hear that. But you're more than welcome to stay with us tonight, really. It must be a little creepy up there. The only company you have is Jolie." Ellie let a little laugh escape.

"Who's that?" Dana felt a tingle. Did she have a house-keeper tucked away in some dusty vestibule?

"Oh, I thought you knew. But then again, I suppose

nobody really wants to advertise it. It's just common knowledge if you live in these parts – you know what I'm saying."

"Uh-huh," Dana said, wishing she'd get on with it.

"Jolie's pretty much of a wild child. When she was five years old, her parents, both of them, were killed in an accident. Jolie was in her car seat just right – in the back in the middle, you know – and she got one little bruise on her forehead and that was all. If her parents had been wearing their seatbelts, they say, they probably would have been just as lucky. You have yours on, don't you, dear? Good. I know it's law in California, isn't it? Well, just as well, and I believe that.

"So Jolie's folks weren't so lucky. It was a van. Ran the stop sign where Fargo crosses 431, that's just above Incline. Hit the car right in the side. It spun all the way around in traffic and got hit again on the other side. Her mom went into the windshield, broke her neck, died instantly. Her dad was thrown from the car. He died on the road." Ellie concentrated on the opposite lane then swung out and passed a slow-moving trailer.

"Jolie's aunt and uncle live just outside Lapis. They had two kids themselves, but they went through the official proceedings and legally adopted the child. Now the accident was seven, almost eight years ago. Nobody knows how much the poor thing saw, but she'll never be right. For the most part, she runs away from home and stays in the woods up here. Her foster parents, bless their hearts, can't hold her. The best they can do is wait for the phone to ring. Neighbours here all know Jolie, and they call if they spot her. Then her aunt and uncle come out and pick her up – if she's in the mood to go home, that is."

"Does she sleep out in the woods?"

"Warm nights, I hear she does sometimes. But mostly she can work her way back home. I don't think anybody knows the woods around here better than Jolie. You should see her – she covers ground quick as a little bobcat."

"I wonder if I should put out something to eat," Dana said, almost seriously.

124

"Ha! I think Whit's tried that. He's drawn her half a dozen times. What I mean is, he's drawn his idea of her – he's never seen her once. I think she's his little nymphet fantasy or something. Men." Ellie chuckled again, a little wistfully.

Dana laughed, to agree. She looked out the window, down the hill at the woods heavy enough to hide anyone. She imagined for a moment that if she ever had a child, it would turn out something like that, wild-willed and cunning. She hoped she would spot Jolie one day. Maybe she should put something out. But if she did, she'd probably attract more raccoons than little girls. Jolie and herself, Dana thought, both alone in the woods. Then she asked Ellie about Whit, and the conversation went on to Louis and Kenji, and soon they arrived at the gallery in King's Beach.

"I like them, I really do," Ellie repeated as they browsed the canvases. Dana couldn't tell whether she was being honest or just trying to be nice because the expedition had been Dana's idea.

Actually, Ellie could never look at paintings without imagining how they would match certain decors – rooms in her house, to be specific. She didn't say so, but that's what she meant when she liked some and didn't like others.

Dana didn't care for most of them, so she guessed Ellie was being nice. It wasn't the subject that bothered her. For the most part, they were impressions of the lake and its surroundings, just stylised enough to call attention to the painter, recognisable enough to be saleable decorations. It was the nervous energy, a tense interplay among the colours, that Dana found upsetting. Ducks lifting from the lake pulled their paddle feet out in dazzling fountains of spray. Somehow the water and sky had become yellow and orange that almost hurt the eyes. The look was derivative of a popular painter who did mostly athletes in action, their faces and bodies jumpy mosaics or high-speed smears of yellow and red. His name, like a space movie that was once briefly popular, escaped her at the moment.

A card and gift counter was situated at the front of the

gallery, and the hanging filled the long room behind it. As Dana and Ellie worked their way around, they noticed that the baffle at the end of the room partly concealed another area, a dog-leg in the gallery that created a more intimate space.

"Who did these?" Ellie asked.

"The same, I think." Dana checked the signature: Aldahl.

She felt drawn from one picture to the next: a view of the lake again, but suddenly cool; a misty cove; an impressionistic hillside with patches of chaparral; a dim shoreline with a single cottage light.

"Not very chipper, is he?" Ellie commented from the opposite wall.

Dana crossed over and read the title: "Self Portrait". The face was an outline, a curving framework of blue and brown. Although they weren't rendered completely, only the eyes seemed finished. The colour that filled them was oddly luminous, disconcerting, eyes of mercury.

What could you *do* with it? Ellie was thinking.

Dana stared at it, fascinated by the spare but oddly sensual outline and strange colours. The subject was lonely, she thought, a little creepy perhaps, but at least human. It was human. Paintings couldn't be done by machines. It had to be human, even those eyes.

"Paintings are like confessions, are they not?" The voice seemed to slip into Dana's thoughts, the way the figure behind them had slipped in undetected.

"You gave me a start!" Ellie scolded, slapping the man's sleeve. She was giggling nervously.

"I am sorry, ladies," Noah Taggart said. "That was not my intention."

"Oh, you're forgiven, I suppose." Ellie was smiling coyly.

"Thank you, Mrs Norwood."

"Ellie, please."

"Ellie," he said, a smile on his rough face briefly, like a light. "And Mrs Ferrin, my near-neighbour, how have you been in the great house?"

Dana looked up at Taggart, and he seemed looser, more

affable, more attractive than he had the evening of Kenji's party. His shirt was open at the throat, a light shirt, fine cotton or silk with an Italian-looking stripe, copper and gold. His smoking jacket was camel-coloured raw silk.

"Fine," she said, thinking it wasn't enough. "Wonderful. We're loving it."

Taggart nodded, but as Dana looked into his eyes, she had the sense that he could see straight into her loneliness. She thought she was giving herself away. He turned his attention back to the pictures. She remembered what he had said.

"Confessions?" she asked suddenly.

"Excuse me?"

"You said paintings are like confessions."

Taggart smiled.

"Only if they're good, true. They can be like secrets, something you must tell if you want to make yourself fully understood, something that defies being said in any other way."

Dana nodded, not following entirely. Lies, she was thinking without really knowing why. Why did the paintings seem to her like lies? Was it the paintings or Noah Taggart?

"This is an interesting exhibit, don't you think?" he went on. "Terry's work has been evolving in new directions."

"You know him, then," Dana said.

"We met at one of his hangings a year or so ago. He was quite concerned with selling work then. Happily, when his career began to flourish, he had the freedom to do more insightful pieces. I was pleased to see the change." He looked at Dana. "Painting is an old love of mine."

He seemed to be looking so intently that Dana wondered what it meant. Was he expecting a reply? Was he hinting that he had other old loves too, while demonstrating clearly that he was suave enough to sweep any young thing off her feet? She felt a little dizzy.

"You must paint too, then," Ellie chimed in.

"As a matter of fact, yes. Nothing of professional calibre, I assure you. It's a diversion for me as well as a way of training myself to see. Few of us possess natural talent, but we can all learn to see."

127

Dana felt that he was practising on her, seeing inside her in some way.

"If perhaps you ladies have time," he continued, "I'd be pleased to show you my work."

"That sounds exciting," Ellie brightened and turned to Dana.

It sounded intriguing to Dana too. She knew it was silly, but the way Taggart looked at her made her want Louis there.

"I would like to see your paintings – very much. I'm sure my husband would be interested too. He had to return to the city for a couple of days, but I expect him back tomorrow. Do you think we could all come to see them in a day or two?"

"Of course." He nodded cordially and produced personal cards for them both from his breast pocket. "Please do telephone. And I hope your husband is able to come. Louis, isn't it?" A smile played on his lips for a moment.

"Yes," Dana said. "Yes, it is."

It stuck in her mind, a minor annoyance. It was there as they were leaving the gallery and, as she was having coffee with Ellie later, it kept surfacing in her thoughts. She was replaying Kenji's party. It was the only place he could have met Louis. How else could Noah Taggart have known his name? They must have been introduced there. She tried to remember them standing together but couldn't. Nevertheless, they must have, if just for a moment. It took a while for Dana to assure herself of that because she was sure she would have seen them, and she would have remembered.

17

Light streamed in through the tall windows in Noah Taggart's studio. It was late afternoon light, and it fell brutally on the canvases arranged along the wall. The intensity of it was what Taggart relished. It suited his mood.

128

He had been right! From the beginning he had been right about Dana Ferrin. At the gathering at Kenji's house, there had been so many in the room, so many pulses and emanations to sort through. In the gallery he had been able to sense her clearly, to read her without distractions. She was well prepared.

He went to the window and raised it the foot or so until it stuck. It smelled musty in the old room and it would, regardless of the window.

He turned and surveyed the pictures, the sun reflecting from the hard, brittle surfaces of the paint. He smiled at the happy accident, how the light was like the light in the settings he painted, stark mountainscapes, snow-capped, under unadulterated sun.

He had been correct. He was not deceiving himself. Nevertheless, his need was strong. It could be colouring his judgement.

He paced back to the far wall of the studio and regarded the pictures again. Each rugged setting seemed to be telling him the same thing.

His need to share the burden was great. But he must be careful. He must, above all else, be right. To share with anyone meant that he would possess her, take her unto himself. Such possessions could, as he had learned, destroy. The one he desired most could be crushed, mutilated. He must be right.

Mara had crumpled, withered in his grip. The burden had been too great. He had deceived himself into believing that she had been prepared. Her beauty had misled him — and his own need.

Now who was Dana Ferrin but Mara's shadow? They were much alike, he knew. But there was a difference also, a crucial one. Some interlacing of events in Dana's life had readied her. A structure within her had been jarred and fractured, ready to be healed much stronger than before, realigned in a new pattern. He had seen it from the start. He had read the signs in her eyes and hands, the way her charges flickered like static from inside. That she had been intended for another purpose was a minor matter. Plans

129

were details, subject to change. He was correct, he assured himself again. She would be the one.

She was fresh in his memory. Her body would be supple to the touch. Her dark eyes were wide, open to possibility. Her quickness betrayed her – a part of her seemed always to be moving, light and shadow continually alternating in her eyes, showing her ill at ease with her own body, the condition of her spirit. Soon she would see what Taggart saw in her; potential as great or greater than any other. Or she could be made to see.

He was looking at one of the paintings in particular, and it brought him back to himself. How befitting it was, he thought with a sardonic laugh. The palette was sharp white and bitter slate and shades of grey. The crags were swept by wind and blown needles of glittering ice. What an accurate reflection of himself, what an unsolicited confession. Taggart's loneliness gusted and whirled inside him.

The need. He had toiled with it for so long. As they inevitably did, his need and his loneliness fuelled rage. It was a relief to feel the rage begin as he paced the studio from end to end before the paintings, the evidence of his solitude and yearning. It was like rescue. He could use rage to pull himself up from the remorseless pit that opened when the loneliness came. He could use it like a climber's rope and piton on the face of a mountain.

He would survive, as he always had. The flat yellow sunlight struck one side of his face. He realised that he had been afraid. Instinct had protected him from the possibility, but now he admitted it to himself. The chance to share had come again. No longer sure of its target, the rage was writhing inside him. The side of Noah Taggart's face was whitish-grey, like granite, in the merciless light from the window.

18

Dana glanced at herself in the rearview mirror. She didn't like what she saw. It reminded her of looking in the bathroom mirror that morning – the dark rings around her eyes. The fact that she volunteered to drive because she knew he was tired struck her as humorous in a grim way. She just hoped he didn't notice. He didn't seem to.

"Ah, yes," Louis opined. "Nothing like the comforts of the country. That's it for the rest of the trip, too. I'm sure they won't need me again. They said don't call for a couple of days. Even then, it's just kind of a formality. Working late that night really bailed them out, you know? I'm glad I did it. It turned out okay."

"That's great," Dana said and she meant it. It was a relief to have him back. They still had most of a week to go. Now maybe the trip would seem like fun again. At least maybe she would get some sleep. "Wow," she said. "How much farther can it be?"

Louis checked the map of the lake in the back of the *Tahoe Summer Fun* paper. When they had started the drive to the South Shore casino strip that afternoon, they had the irrational idea that half an hour would get them there. Later, in the insert entitled "Tahoe Facts", Louis read that although the lake was twenty-two miles long, the shoreline was seventy-one, and more than half of that lay on the west shore, on winding roads, the route they had taken to the south. Still, they had no reason to rush, and the views of the deep coves around the lake, bordered by lush woods, were spectacular.

"Okay, we just passed Pope Beach and that's the Highway 50 junction coming up. We're almost there, less than five minutes."

Louis had been thinking of saying something. He knew it was stupid, but why not? She might appreciate it.

"So, what all haven't you told me about your girl's night out?"

"What?"

"Your bachelorette weekend. You know, the really big night life: King's Beach, Tahoe Vista. Meet any lifeguards?"

"No." She didn't look amused.

"No?"

"Well, if you must know . . ."

He was spellbound.

131

"The extent of my wild time was going to an art gallery with Ellie. We ran into Noah Taggart."

"Wow, the Grand Duke of Lapis. How did you handle it?" She was surprised at his tone.

"Don't be silly. He's really a very nice, humble man."

"Uh-huh." He drummed his fingers on his knee.

"Really. He just takes getting used to."

"I believe you," he said. "Okay, just go straight now."

Louis sat up and kept Dana from angling on to the highway that would lead to Sacramento. He didn't know exactly what about Taggart made him uncomfortable. The local idol worship was certainly part of it, but not all.

Soon the traffic began to jam, and the casino hotels of the South Shore appeared, decked in white lights under the orange sky. Billboards advertised $19.95 per person per night. As they rolled down the main drag, signs and marquees lit up the street like artificial day. The casino doors were open wide, and each of them looked like its own carnival with red and gold slots visible inside and tourists crowding in or gawking from the sidewalk.

They passed Caesar's and Harvey's and Dell Webb's High Sierra and decided on Harrah's, towards the end of the line. Dana pulled into a parking lot the size of the Rose Bowl, and they walked in on a splurge of cheap red carpet through the side door.

She didn't need the lights. They swam in from every direction; all the hanging signs that marked the keno tables and baccarat, kinetic videogame monitors displaying electronic poker, bright white lights on the spinning roulette wheels and the red chips and the cards in their primary colours on the green felt tables. She was not in the mood for visual assault. Idiot, she thought, what did you expect? She knew she should make the best of it.

"What do you think?" she ventured. He was looking similarly shell-shocked, staring down into the sunken gaming floor. They watched a woman in a wheelchair feed a coin to a slot and pull the arm down. Again. Again.

"A primitive paradise," he said, "virtually unspoiled. Hey, you okay?"

Dana caught a glimpse of her washed-out self in the mirrored wall.

"Sure. Really, I am. Just a little tired. Want to try one?"

"One what?"

She pointed to the quarter slots. He fished in his pocket, put on his poker face, and winked. They descended the few steps to the machines that waited in lines like jolly robots. Gamers pulled the levers down and the cylinders whirled, three fruits chasing one another for a match.

"You're probably right," he said cryptically then popped in a quarter and pulled the arm down. He knew she had been put off by his attitude for the last fifteen minutes. She just looked at him.

"About Taggart," he went on. "He's probably harmless enough."

"Sure he is. He even invited Ellie and us over to his place to see some of his paintings. I think we should go. He lives just up the hill somewhere."

Louis wasn't saying anything. He popped another quarter and pulled.

"You're a victim of generational mentality, you know?" She had only meant to tease him, but it sounded strident, and she knew it was because she was tired and mad that she was tired. Whatever she was in the mood for, it wasn't an argument, especially since he had just got back.

He didn't say anything, looked around, looked back down, fingered his change.

"Fear of old people, huh," he said. He tried to be honest with himself about how much the thought of getting old brought with it a vision of decay and a smell of death.

"You're probably right – again," he said. She looked relieved. "I suppose I should work on that, right? How about this – I'll pay him a visit myself." He didn't know why he said it. It was something like having a brief flash of how short life was.

"You will not," she said.

A metallic rushing sound made their skins jump. Three machines away, quarters charged down a silver chute. A sixtyish woman in white stretch pants held a pail the size of a coffee can to the mouth of it, catching the avalanche. She ground gum, taking it in her stride.

"Don't believe me, eh?" he said, returning to the subject of Taggart. "I know – I'll bet you everything you're about to win on the next pull." He held out a quarter between thumb and forefinger.

"You're on."

As Dana held the quarter up to the slot, she realised they should go to another row of machines because luck wouldn't strike again so close. But they had been lucky once before, hadn't they? She was surprised that remembering that night didn't excite her any more. She was just tired. She dropped the quarter and pulled the silver arm down and watched the cylinder of bright fruit spin into a blur.

Bert Hathaway checked his watch and checked the blackjack table. Watch out for devices. As far as card counters, there wasn't much you could do. Julian was there, for example. Easy Julian, they called him. It came from the night after his big score. All the cashiers threw up their hands at the same time when he came in to play again. "Take it easy, Julian" was what they said. They had rehearsed it, kind of in honour of him. The guy was probably a genius or something. How he could count cards that fast Bert would never know.

What could you do with Julian, anyway? Just speak to him in private if things started to get out of hand. Some would listen to that, some wouldn't. Julian listened. He was no stupid genius. Other than that, his winning was good for business, good advertising. Best advertising you could have, as a matter of fact, making it look like any dumb jerk could do it. They didn't know Julian was a genius. Good thing fucking geniuses were rare, Bert thought, stupid or otherwise. If there were very many of them, a lot more people would be out of a job, including him.

He had only taken the job as a floor walker for the summer. He was saving to train as a computer tech. Inside of a week it got boring. Not as boring as the 7-Eleven, but

134

pretty bad. Still, he told himself, it wasn't hard, and it was good because it gave you time to think. About what, Bert couldn't say in so many words. Now he was thinking he had less than three hours until the end of his shift at eleven.

He glanced down the aisle of Jumbo Poker machines. A guy at the end caught his eye. Nothing special about him, really. Short dark hair, average build, yellow shirt, probably one of those little alligators on it. Just something about the way he was leaning against the Lady of the House machine: the big one everybody looked at and almost nobody ever played. Bert decided to walk over there.

As he got closer, the man took a drag from a cigarette. Then he went on doing what he did before, which was stare down the long main aisle towards the far end of the floor. As Bert passed him, their eyes met for a second and the man nodded. He looked like he was casing the whole place, but Bert didn't actually see him do anything funny.

He wondered if they were watching the guy through the tilted windows of one-way glass all around the top of the wall. He moved a few machines away and played Jumbo Poker for a while, checking him all the time from the corner of his eye. He wasn't doing anything, just leaning against the Lady and looking.

Bert finished a hand. Oh well, he thought, that's just the way it is sometimes. The guy was waiting for somebody or waiting to get lucky, like every other dumb jerk. Waiting for luck to bite him in the ass. Lucky for him he was leaning on the Lady of the House. If it had been another one, he might have asked the guy to move. They ought to take that machine out, Bert thought as he got up. By the time he checked the man once more and headed for the keno tables, he was convinced he was okay. He was just some guy biding his time.

Leaning his shoulder against the arcade machine, Brian Thomas watched the row of quarter slots at the far end of the floor. More precisely, he watched Louis and Dana walking among them. They had tried two. They were trying another. He put his hand to his hip pocket and rested it there, on the square bulge of his wallet. Had Dana changed?

He couldn't see her face clearly. Was she still like the picture in his pocket and in his mind? He knew what he wanted and he wanted her to be like that. Exactly.

Brian watched them go side by side up the short carpeted stairs. He took a drag on his cigarette and held it until they exited into the bright lights outside the open door and turned away into the night crowd.

19

Frieda Beckman turned away from the dining-room window and faced Noah Taggart across the long dark table. She was ready, she told herself. She would say it all, and when she was done, it would help to close the distance. She would help to return him to himself. It was her role. She took a sip of coffee and centred the gold-rimmed cup on the saucer.

"Why don't you sit down, Frieda?" Taggart said from his chair at the far end of the table.

She felt a dip in her stomach. Whatever he said could unnerve. She smoothed it over inside in her professional way, like taking a deep breath without really taking one.

She pulled out a chair and sat down. Noah looked fatigued. His eyes seemed cold. On top of a credenza behind him a bronze statue of a stallion reared, head back, mane whipping. Taggart was waiting, saying nothing. From his living room she could hear a clock.

"Noah, I want to talk to you as a friend, as someone who knows you as well as anyone."

His face was still.

"You've been unhappy, it's obvious. You're stuck. The conflict you're in is unhealthy. I fear it will affect you in other ways."

He said nothing, showed nothing. He was like a resistant client. She reminded herself to keep her composure.

"There's a distance growing around you, between us. A distraction. It hurts me – "

"Are we talking about you or me?"

The interruption felt like a knife. He sat and waited. He was like a stone, she thought. He must be moved.

"It hurts me to watch you belittle yourself. This one you've become fixed on, she's a lesser soul. I'm afraid it's becoming obsessional. You can't see yourself. You're actually pitiable but I don't want to pity you. I want to help you work through your conflict."

"Oh yes, conflict is a disease to you."

"Not necessarily. But obsession is. Its source is a delusion. There are forms you've invented which simply cannot be attained. You've invented them for that reason." She was talking too fast, she knew, but she had to go on.

"The target of your desire doesn't exist. She's a phantom of your own making, a form only – unattainable – an archetype. You can't see her – " She tilted the edge of her saucer inadvertently and it clattered back on the table. "You can't see her as she is at all. It's impossible for you to see anything clearly, even yourself. If you could see yourself, you would laugh – "

"Enough!" He slammed the table, and the cup and saucer jumped. The slap went through her. She was suddenly in a tiny boat far out at sea and the sound was a thunderclap.

"In all your learning," Taggart's voice started deep in his chest, "you have learned so little. Least of all about desire. Who are you," he spoke with menacing slowness, each word falling like a weight, "to lecture me?"

Frieda was unable to speak. Inside she was fluttering. She felt bound to her chair, even as Taggart was rising.

"It would be better, Frieda, to examine your own desires, small though they may be. They seem to have made no small difference for you." A cold smile was beginning as he rounded the corner of the table, long fingers of one hand still resting on the wood.

"Let me remind you of your desire when I found you. No doubt you think of it as 'when we met'. One of your little delusions, and I have no desire to indulge it. When I found you – as I found all the others – do you remember what you wanted for your practice, how great that desire

137

seemed? I daresay you do not because you have it now. Perhaps it will help to remember what you were willing to do for it."

Her heart was beating fast, skipping like a record missing grooves. Taggart took a step closer.

"You do remember that, don't you?" he continued, knowing exactly where to strike, pressing the point home.

"I see you do," he said, confirming for Frieda what she feared, that the blank white terror of her own memories was showing in her face.

"Perhaps you recall it every day of your life," he went on, moving closer. "You'll be relieved to know, Frieda, that almost no one talks about him any more. Michael, that was your husband's name, wasn't it? He's become just one more of the stories, one of those who died in the lake, his body never found. Never found because bodies do not float — they sink in the cold centre, in a thousand feet of water. Water so cold that the bodies are preserved, no gases ever forming to buoy them upwards." He was above her. His breath smelled like wet ashes.

"Imagine the bodies in those waters so deep, my dear Frieda. All those who were never recovered, wide-eyed in their deep dance on the currents, rising and falling. Imagine Michael among them there, precisely there, one thousand feet below the centre of the lake where you rode with him. Where you took him as the jackal takes the monkey. With strength I gave you. No one else." His large hand descended like a claw on to the arm of the chair. He was leaning over her, bending down.

The memory was flowing through her again. After twelve years the cold currents of the dream still chilled her. Michael's cries for help came again, the cries which only she had heard in the middle of Lake Tahoe as she stood in the open boat, alone, still throbbing with the power of Taggart. Michael's eyes told her: she had become something he had never known. He was thrashing, throwing spray in all directions, choking down, the lake covering him like a shroud.

"Yes," Taggart said, inches from her face, inspecting her

138

features as though checking for evidence of life. "I see you do recall."

He stood up slowly and walked to a hutch along the side wall. Heavy iron candlesticks sat on the front of it, at either end. He stood with his back towards her, but she could see him silently fingering one.

"When you returned to shore," he went on, still facing away, "you came back to success you never dared dream of. Wasn't that your . . .?" He turned to face her. "Desire? Your . . . obsession? Have you not reaped the rewards?" His fingers wrapped around the heavy black casting.

"Ask yourself, Frieda, are desires and deeds like these fuelled by delusions? Are they fired by the tiny emotional frictions of your psychology? You dare to speak to me of desire. And obsession . . ." Taggart's hand was tightening around the candlestick, his fingers white against the black.

Suddenly he laughed. It was a ragged, throaty laugh, tossed aside. He let the candlestick go and returned to the far end of the table. He faced her with a level stare.

"And look at yourself. What do you imagine brought you here today, so full of fears and helpless as a child? Your desires and needs, perhaps, not mine? Can it be, Frieda, that you are much more a prisoner of longing than I?"

She wanted to answer. She tried to summon a response, but she had too little left. She was humiliated, punished. Her hand, which had slipped away from the coffee cup, lay white and inert on the table. She found herself in a long, dreadful silence, only waiting, listening to her own fast, hollow breathing.

Taggart turned and left the room abruptly. She heard him stop in the short hall that lead to the kitchen.

What was he going to do to her? There was a table in the hall. She tried to remember if it had a drawer, if the drawer held knives. But that wouldn't be his way, she tried to convince herself.

She should take the chance, try to escape. But could she make the front door? Where was the strength to stand? She was icy emptiness inside. Hollowness. Murderess. If he killed her, what did it matter? She was his anyway, chained to him.

She heard him with the telephone in the short hall. In a moment he stepped back into the room and watched her, the receiver to his ear.

"Hello, Daniel," he said, eyeing her coolly. "This is Noah Taggart. Frieda wants you to pick her up. I think it's best that she doesn't drive. She tried to do too much and now she isn't feeling well. Not well at all."

PART III
Madonna and Child

20

The bed was shaking. Then the room was shaking. As Dana's eyes opened, the room was shaking. Then she saw him.

Louis was propped on one elbow, shaking her shoulder, shaking her awake. She had been in a dream, and in the next second she knew that when he would ask, she dared not tell him.

"You okay?" he was saying, and his eyes were funny. Dana's unconscious screams had jerked him awake like a hook in his insides. "That was some dream. You okay?"

She nodded, sitting up, rubbing her forehead. Louis put his arm around her. The light in the bedroom was grey. Dana thought dawn was hours off before she checked the clock and saw that it was nearly eight. Clouds had moved in overnight.

"What was it about?" he asked, as expected.

"I can't really remember," she said. "There was a dog and he was chasing me, or something stupid. I really screamed, huh? Sorry I woke you up. It was nothing really."

"It didn't sound like nothing." He was rubbing the middle of her back. "Say, I have an idea. It looks like it's going to rain today. What if I make a fire and bring up breakfast and we stay in bed as long as we want?"

"Great, with one exception. I'll make the breakfast," she insisted, feeling as she started to get up that she had weights on.

"You sure? I can do it."

"Absolutely." She was pulling on her robe. "You even rate an omelette if you're nice."

All the time Dana was cleaning up and going through

the motions of making their breakfast in bed, a task which ordinarily would have made her blissfully happy, she kept fighting thoughts of the dream. Her brain had been running since the episode with the car, but nothing had been as bad as last night.

It had begun like the oppressive thing at the lake with Louis, but soon she was drowning. It was the only way she could think of it, even though it had nothing to do with water. It was a heavy shadow like thick smoke. It settled down on her, surrounded her like sickly sweet gas, suffocating. Inside the shadow was a frightful sound, like rushing wind. She heard others too – a raspy low tone like a long deep vowel, and ones that made her cringe, like tiny cries. While she was in the dream, Dana had no sense that she could ride it out, or call out to rescue herself, or even scream herself awake. She couldn't remember how she had done it, or what was happening just before she had. She did recall that the most terrifying part was not the oppressive smoke or even the sounds, but what seemed to be just beyond the smoke, a sombre presence, dreadful, heavy enough to crush the spirit.

Through breakfast she worked on resurrecting her mood, but she could feel herself losing by degrees. Louis had a guide to local attractions and he kept whistling the *Bonanza* theme and talking about visiting the Ponderosa ranch. Even with the fire going in the bedroom, it wasn't enough. Joking along with him was exhausting.

When they were through, he made a big production of not taking the dishes back downstairs, insisting instead on piling them in the hall outside the door, letting the illusion of room service or maids handle them. Dana went into the bathroom, and by the time she returned, she had made up her mind to try it.

"How about this?" she began, slipping back into bed, trying to keep it light. "What if we catch the Ponderosa tomorrow on the way home?"

"On the way where?"

"Home."

"I don't get it."

144

"I mean we could go back early. We'd have time to enjoy the city. How many times have we wanted to take the ferry to Angel Island?" She watched him closely and smiled. Don't be too heavy, she was thinking. Don't say too much.

"Are you crazy?" He sat up and stared at her. Then he got out of bed and stared. "We've got less than a week left here anyway. We don't exactly have plans to do this every month."

He paced to the door and back. Then he looked her over and sat down on the bed again.

"What is it?" he asked quietly. "Something's really bothering you."

"Nothing much. I just thought it would be nice to have some time in the city, that's all. I'd like to be around familiar things again. Is that so crazy? Don't you feel disconnected up here?"

"No, not really. Maybe we should have a few people over for drinks. Just Kenji and a couple of friends. And I'm going fishing in a few days, remember? You come too – you'll like it. We still have a lot to do up here. It would be a shame to cut it short, don't you think?"

They both sat in silence for a while and Dana watched the dying fire. She was too tired to fight.

"Okay," she said.

"Why don't you take a nap and you'll feel better. Besides, we can't leave yet. I have some important business to attend to." Louis popped out of bed again. "Where's your address book?"

She just looked at him for a moment.

"In my purse – it's in the bathroom. Why?"

He went in and she heard him rummaging in her bag.

"We have a bet going, remember?" He came back out with her black book open. "I'm about to call your friend, Mr Taggart," he announced.

"You don't have to do that just to please me. I don't care, really," she said. "It'll be a drag for you."

"It will not," he protested. "It wouldn't hurt us to feel a little more connected. You want to come?"

"Not today," she said. Then added, "Tomorrow would

be okay." If they were staying, she thought, she might as well go along since he was being nice. It might even make her feel better about things, but it was hard to imagine.

"Okay, you get some rest. I'll give him a buzz. Be right back."

Dana heard him go down the stairs. It was the last thing she heard for a while. The idea of a nap had made her nervous at first. She didn't want to risk another dream. Nevertheless, as she lay her head on the pillow and watched the low fire, the weight of fatigue pressed all the worry flat and she slept. When she woke, Louis was beside her, reading.

"Hi, sleepy-head. Feeling better?"

"I think so," she nodded, blinking out of the haze. "How did your call go?"

"Fine. He was affable as can be. He invited us both for a drink after dinner. Since he asked, I didn't think I should put him off until tomorrow. Do you think you'll feel like going later on?"

Dana sat up and tried to envision a way she would feel like visiting, but couldn't.

"I think I just want to do some reading today. You mind?"

"No problem. I'll say you're feeling a little sick. Hey, you aren't, are you? You're shivering."

"It's chilly in here," she said, getting up, reaching for her robe on the chair. The fire was out, but Dana knew that wasn't the reason. It was the sense she had again fleetingly, unclear but nonetheless upsetting, the sense of the presence behind the smoke.

Louis knocked for the second time and waited. The plaque beside the mailbox at the end of the drive had read "Dunn's Crest", but aside from that, he could have wondered if he had the wrong place.

He stepped back from the door and looked up the rugged face of the old frame house. Empty windows. Was Taggart asleep? The sky behind the house was darkening orange, and he noticed a hawk or buzzard circling in the distance. He checked his watch. Two past eight.

146

It was a power play of some kind. Louis didn't like being jerked around by the local celeb. He raised his hand again, ready to pound with the bottom of his fist. Suddenly the door opened, catching him off balance.

"Ah, Louis, I beg your pardon. I was in the nether reaches of the house." Taggart extended his hand, smiling cordially. "Your lovely wife couldn't come?"

"I'm afraid she's a little under the weather."

"I'm sorry to hear that. Perhaps another time. Please come in."

Taggart had clasped his hand with both hands, and he had the strange sensation that he was being drawn in across the transom. Finally Taggart released him and pushed the heavy door shut.

"I'm so pleased you decided to visit me." The old man sounded sincere. "I so seldom have guests up here. It's rather far for most people. Fortunately, we live on the same hill." He led Louis out of the foyer into the entrance hall beside the stairs.

"Yes, fortunately," Louis said. Old money and good taste, he was thinking as they made their way down the hall. Nothing ostentatious, everything fine. An oriental runner led past low bookcases, dark wood, cherry. A spreading fern sat at the end of the first. On another, a crystal falcon statuette sparkled softly as they passed, head turned regally to the side.

"I'm quite out of practice at making new acquaintances. I was wondering if I could interest you in a few souvenirs of my travels."

"I'd be delighted. Kenji said you had taken some pretty extensive treks. You're a climber too, I understand?"

"Was, I'm afraid. The boots in the closet haven't touched a mountain for twenty years."

Taggart pushed open a door and nodded, and Louis stepped past him into a large, curious room. Two stuffed chairs and two leather wing chairs around a circular coffee table gave it a cosy denlike feel, as did the fireplace on the far wall, but as the chimney drew Louis's eye up, he realised how high the beamed ceiling was. He imagined for

147

a moment that he could have been standing under a great inverted boat, a feeling he used to have in church, looking up at the high ceiling of the nave.

The room, though large, felt full. It was a personal museum, abundantly stocked with artifacts. Louis was drawn to the rows of photographs on the walls.

"Those are bushmen of the Australian outback," the old man volunteered. Louis was studying a picture of a younger Taggart in short sleeves and shorts surrounded by Aborigines, posing stiffly with their spears. "We were great friends by the time I left," he went on. "I never hit it off with their neighbours in the next bush, but it was just as well. They still practised cannibalism – avidly, I'm afraid."

The photos continued around the walls like a world travelogue in black and white slides: a kayak between icebergs, a peak in the Italian Alps, a camel caravan swirled with dust, dense jungle Taggart identified as Sumatra. Even the simple frames were like samples of the world's woods; teak and cherry and rosewood and bamboo.

Louis estimated sixty or seventy photographs on the three walls. How could one man have done so much? Some of the shots looked ancient, clouded with decades of mist.

"What's this one? It looks like it's from the turn of the century."

Louis was actually thinking it was older. The white men stood in khaki and safari helmets beside tents pitched on a beach. Smoke drifted sideways from a fire in front of them, and a short distance behind the tents, the jungle was a dark line. Louis spotted the one who must have been Taggart, off to the side, with one of the black guides or bearers. But how could it have been? The photo was eighty years old or older, but the man looked middle-aged. Still, the prominent brows and jaw were exactly the same.

"You're quite right," Taggart said. "It was taken in 1894. My father was part of this expedition down the Niger." He pointed to the man on the side. "Quite a restless soul also. He was in the import-export business. Today he could claim trips to Africa and the Far East as deductions. Of course,

then there was no deduction because there was no tax."
Taggart laughed.

"Would you join me in a Madeira, Louis?" He indicated
one of the wing chairs, and Louis sat as he retrieved a crystal
decanter from the mantel and glasses from the sideboard.

"A good Madeira never ages to senility, so they say."
Taggart poured two glasses and raised one.

"To your finding a second home in Alpenhurst. May
you enjoy it so much that we become . . . regular neighbours."

They touched glasses. The Madeira tasted sweet-strong
to Louis, and complex. The bouquet and flavour brought
a warm rush to his chest.

"Are you familiar with Madeiras? I believe a fine Madeira
is the equal of any port. It is made by the *solera* method.
The wine passes from barrel to barrel as it ages over years.
Please." He uncovered a humidor on the table between
them, and the aroma of fresh tobacco rose from it. Louis
took a cigar and Taggart lit it, then took one for himself.

"The grapes must be removed from each cask at precisely
the proper time," he went on. "Too little time or too much
produces a Madeira that is either undistinguished or too
sweet. A successful Madeira is the result of timing, which,
in turn, is a matter of intuition and decisiveness. Few people
possess both in equal measure."

He is smooth, Louis thought. He was impressed again
with Taggart's clothes; the fine pink shirt with white collar
and the charcoal jacket. Louis followed a draw on the cigar
with another sip of the wine. They blended perfectly.
Taggart asked how he and Dana were enjoying the house,
and while they talked about Alpenhurst, Louis had a chance
to survey the rest of the treasures in the room.

Close to the door, a huge glass globe, nearly three feet
in diameter, was mounted in a wooden housing. The three
legs of the housing stood on a zebra-skin rug, and on the
wall behind the globe hung a tribal mask, black with
white eyes and an orange diamond-shaped mouth. On the
opposite wall were a dark skin shield with leather quiver
and arrows, beside the shield a case of bright red beads,

149

a brace of flintlock pistols mounted to the side. Half a dozen paintings and prints filled the fireplace wall, and one large print in a heavy frame was especially disturbing, a battle scene from another century, hand-to-hand combat and pistols at point-blank range. Dark wood blades of a ceiling fan rotated slowly above their heads.

Louis thought about the room, what it meant. Experience and money. It was another league. Taggart was trying to make him feel at home, though. He was rich, but he was probably just as lonely.

They drank and smoked for a few moments in silence. Outside the tall windows, the sky was nearly dark. Louis felt no pressure to rekindle the conversation. The Madeira was partly responsible. He also felt at ease with Taggart, which he hadn't expected. The old man seemed quiet and fatherly and a little sad. How did one arrive? Louis mused. How did one acquire the wherewithal to travel the globe, or even buy a glass one the size of Taggart's? Then he remembered.

"Kenji said you had been in the mining business."

Taggart smiled and nodded and said nothing for a moment, and Louis felt he had been waiting for the question.

"Gold and diamonds," he said, "in the days when fortunes could still be made in South Africa. All that has changed now. It was a matter of fortuitous timing." Louis thought of what he had said about intuition and the capacity to decide and act. "Good fortune was the other player. Fate, chance, call it what you will."

Their eyes locked for an instant and Louis felt slightly dizzy. Taggart looked down, and Louis's line of sight followed, to the decanter. Taggart removed the stopper and refilled the glasses.

"Have you ever noticed," he went on, "that some people seem to lead, shall we say, charmed lives while others – the great majority – do not? And isn't it interesting that so many imagine themselves called to wealth or power or position, but so few are chosen?"

Louis wondered what he was doing. Was it going to

be a pre-senile rap, rehashing his own successes? Was it some lecture he had delivered to son-surrogates a thousand times?

"It isn't a matter of force of will," he continued, "or skill or talent, really. These play a role, but they determine nothing by themselves. Otherwise, more dogged workers would be millionaires – then there would be no workers." He chuckled. "Every aspiring talent would be a star."

So, Louis was thinking but didn't say it. Taggart smiled to himself and nodded and looked down into the decanter. Then he looked up.

"Beyond talent or skill, success is a condition of balance, how events can lean one way in the balance or another. How these events seem tailored to the plans of some but run violently contrary to the will of others."

Taggart hadn't moved, but he looked different. His eyes had hardened, and Louis felt slowed by them, almost drugged. No trace of a smile remained, and when he spoke again, his voice was grave.

"Desire alone, wishes alone, are the wages of the powerless. Desire alone profits nothing, as any schoolboy with some unattainable nymph in his heart well knows. Or as the everyday worker knows, estranged from his job and remote from those with power and means who control his destiny."

Louis's job returned in memory, complete with the loathing he usually tried to deny. He felt nailed, pinned down by Taggart's stare.

"Do you believe for an instant," the old man continued, "that by the force of your own will, your own striving, you can bend the course of events to fit your small desire – when everywhere, around all our lives, events are rushing like a torrent, like a cascade, caring nothing for our puny wishes, heading only towards their own ends, which we are powerless to foretell?" Taggart rose and turned to the mantel.

"If we could realise our ends so simply, don't you suppose that we would find contentment everywhere, not the frustration and violent counterpoint that fill the daily news?

151

Isn't it true that if the keys to happiness could be found in a grab bag of dedicated effort and glib 'positive attitude', then there would be no tortured ghosts of our true selves to hide – the agony that Goya painted – no silent howlers in the dark?" It seemed to take him for ever to speak the words. Taggart was looking at the large print in the gold frame. As he turned around again, Louis realised that the old man had seen him looking at the picture although he seemed not to have noticed at the time.

Louis wanted another drink but stopped himself. His second glass was nearly empty.

"Desire alone does not alter the course of our lives, Louis. Wishing and striving are of little use, even though most behave as though they could take their lives in hand and shape them to their ends like balls of clay." Taggart smiled again, as though the insight brought him a kind of grim pleasure.

"Chance is the real artist," he said softly. He stepped to the side of Louis's chair, then behind it. "And chance can be influenced. Only a bit is enough. Chance can become opportunity as easily as not, if you have the edge."

Taggart's voice from behind sounded as though it were coming through earphones, happening inside Louis's own head. He could feel the old man leaning closer. His hands grasped both sides of the tall wing chair.

"Haven't you wished so often that you had it, Louis – the edge in the balance?"

He said it and was silent and to Louis it was as though he had opened a forbidden door. Thoughts of Dana strayed in, of their careers and the sad imbalance of their incomes, of Kenji's enviable house and his lifelines to freedom and self-respect, of his own helplessness in a job he had defaulted into more than chosen. Taggart's smooth voice had laid him open to the punch. Two large hands gently patted the sides of the chair.

"How does one acquire the edge, then, Louis, if it can be acquired at all? Part of the answer is that it can, certainly. There's nothing mysterious about it, really. One must simply become . . . receptive." He stepped slowly

152

back to his chair and sat down. "It only requires making yourself available. Think of it as answering when opportunity knocks." He stared and his eyes were cold and hard. "Think of it as answering without hesitation when you are called."

How? Louis was thinking. He felt that he would be able to ask – the word would form if he wanted it, but it did not. A sinking feeling was stopping him. He was slipping into a trap. The old geezer had dug a pit for him with every word.

He lowered his glass to the table. The cigar was dead in his hand, and as he tried to get up, he dropped it on the table and it rolled. His head swam. Taggart sat watching.

Standing was like toiling against invisible ropes. Some snapped and some remained. His head was higher than Taggart's but he was wavering. He would not fall in. There was something rotting here.

"I'll be going," he said, stepping sideways around the table. "We have nothing – " Taggart seemed to break it off somehow, even though he was only sitting, watching.

Louis reached the door, but he couldn't enter the hall without stopping for a moment to look back. The old man sat calmly in his finely tailored clothes, head against the back of the wing chair.

"You may call me, Louis," he said and nodded.

Louis turned into the hallway. His head felt no good any more. If he made the car, could he drive? He would walk if he had to.

He was reaching for the front door when he saw it in the low bookcase. He hadn't noticed it before – the size of a child's doll but the colour of sun-baked leather, face black as creosote, a tiny white tooth visible, wings of skin spread and lacquered, angular and pointed, like a bat's.

Taggart listened to the front door opening, and then to the steps on the stairs. He would close the door when his guest was completely gone. He got up and went to the window.

Louis Ferrin was walking out of the front-door light towards his car parked in the shadows where the driveway ended. As Taggart watched him leave, there was nothing in his face to indicate that anything out of the ordinary had happened. The expression on the old weathered face betrayed nothing. It merely was, like the look the spider uses to regard the fly.

"Was that it?" Dana asked.

"Yeah, I told you. We just looked at some old pictures and talked about his world exploits, et cetera, et cetera. The old coot's been around."

Louis lay back on the pillow and rubbed his temples. When he got home, the first move had been to add a glass of burgundy to the Madeira. It had seemed like a good idea at the time.

"Are you sure nothing else happened? You look upset or something."

"No, it's just the wine he had, the Madeira. It was pretty potent. Also, you know, there's something about him."

"What?"

He wanted to tell her, but if he did, he would be writing Taggart off. Part of him wanted to do just that, but he wasn't ready to yet.

"He seemed self-centred, very big on having made his fortune, that kind of thing."

"That's funny, he didn't seem that way to me."

Why couldn't she shut up? He told himself to keep cool.

"Well, he did to me," he said and attacked her with tickles. Dana laughed and rolled on the bed and she felt good to him through the nightgown, at least at first. She felt good enough for him to start something, but in a minute they were only holding each other.

Eventually he turned off the light, and in the hours that followed, he thought of condemning Taggart outright, making a clean breast of everything. Then he thought of money and helplessness and the ease with which Taggart had found that forbidden zone in him and spoken directly to

154

it. Why had Taggart picked him? Had he helped Kenji when he was getting started, with a loan or contacts? Maybe it was no more than that. But Louis couldn't shake the feeling that there was more. If so, he wanted to protect Dana. If there was anything unsavoury about a deal he might make with the old man, he would keep Dana out of it.

He lay staring at the wall as the thoughts replaced one another and then began over again. He didn't know that Dana was watching the other wall, afraid to sleep and dream, as the minutes ticked by. They both lay, back to back, eyes open, listening to the occasional cries of night birds and to the sharp, random creaking of the house.

21

It was late at night when Whit Norwood woke up in his den. He couldn't have been asleep long. The ice cubes in his rum and tonic were approximately the same size as he remembered. The arm raised the glass like a mechanical boom. Glass met lips. Passable. Hell, not bad at all.

He glanced at the pad beside the chair. He had been playing with the series for a while: "Kubla Connie's Pizza Palace". He thought of it as what *Fritz the Cat* should have been. If so, he mused for a grim instant, why the fuck did he fall asleep over it all the time? He hadn't been asleep, he was merely resting his eyes. The ice cubes, priceless little timepieces, were the proof.

An old movie was rolling on the tube. It would stop just long enough to show snapshots of the actors, then it would blink and roll again. He spotted Jimmy Stewart and Doris Day. It was a Hitchcock. That's right, he had seen parts before he had nodded off, and he had been surprised that a decent film was on so late. Hits like *Attack of the Killer Kangaroos* were more typical. What was it? Not *Vertigo*. Not *Rear Window*. He could stop the roll if he switched it off then on with the remote control. He decided not to. He would guess it with a handicap.

Whit had only started to concentrate when he heard something outside. That was it. He didn't just wake up; there had been a noise. He heard it again, a definite rustling, close to the house, maybe as close as the bushes against the wall. It was bigger than a coon, he could tell. Bobcat maybe.

Why not, he thought. He envisioned his picture on the front of the *Bay View*: "Disney Cartoonist Bags Bobcat". He got up and walked carefully, heel to toe, to the drawer beside his bookshelf. He slid it open quietly. He didn't know why, but it always surprised him a little to see it in there. Sleeping. Just waiting for him. A true beaut.

Whit lifted the black Astra 44 revolver. He liked the solid weight of it, not quite three pounds, and balanced. He found the box of bullets in the drawer and began feeding them into the cylinders. He heard it again. Could be a prowler too, he surmised. Think of that photo.

The first three bullets dropped in. The fourth went on the floor, under some damn thing. Fuck it – no time to lose. He grabbed more out of the box. Four, five, six. Snap the cylinder shut.

It was out there, all right, and close. He crossed in front of the TV, wheeled, and practised his aim on the masked mannequin. Then he tiptoed in the front hall to keep from waking Ellie and unlocked the front door softly. He took the first cunning steps outside.

The night was fresh and moist, and he could see a few stars. The day's storm seemed to have passed. Whit stepped away from the front door, off the gravel path and into the quiet wet grass. He listened. Nothing. He crept around the corner, pistol barrel pointing straight up beside his head.

There. The rustle again, close to the den but past it, farther along the wall. He stalked along the line of bushes beside the house. Rum and tonic were doing laps in his system and he was ready for anything. It was the way he felt watching Clint Eastwood in *The Enforcer*. What a stiff that guy was. All the emotions from A to B. A fucking millionaire. He'd seen better acting from a banana slug.

When he drew even with the den window, he heard action again, but away from the house this time, moving steadily towards the woods. It was getting away.

Whit struck out, loping through the thick grass towards the edge of the yard. It was moving, and it kept moving out there in front of him. If it got too far into the woods, that would be a problem.

Upstairs, Ellie rolled over. Whit's not being in the bed wasn't a disappointment, or even a surprise. She was used to his "creative" late nights. You can't let certain things bother you, she had told herself once, if you were going to stay married. If he didn't do the things he did, he wouldn't be the way he was, and that amorphous way she felt fundamentally close to.

Had she given up too much? Her new friend Dana might think so, but Dana was young. Tolerance kept love alive. In fact, if it came down to it, Ellie thought, maybe tolerance was all there was. That's what love reduced to, after a while.

Had Dana and her Louis learned that yet? Ellie hoped they would, for their own sakes. She was a sweet kid, and life, as Ellie had come to know in her bones, was all too short.

Sex, attraction, charm, witty talk, the way you "communicate" – they were like paper money that lost value every year. They didn't mean a tinker's damn if the real thing wasn't there, down deep.

She took a relaxing breath and fanned her arm on the empty side of the king bed like a kid making butterflies in snow. She could just hear the TV down in the den, like their own friendly robot murmuring all is well.

Whit was going hard as he hit the first bushes. He had to stop for a minute. The gun was getting heavy and his heart was charging. He bent over, hands on knees, to catch his breath.

He could hear crickets some distance away, but none close. They had stopped their racket when they heard

157

him coming. He could hear his own breathing but not much more. He stood up slowly. He was feeling a little unsteady, but it would pass. There it was again.

This time it was close, only a few yards ahead in the firs. It was a kind of dragging sound, more like shuffling than like footsteps. He squinted, but it was darker than in the yard, and he could only make out the masses of the tree trunks against the shadows of the brush.

It stopped again. It moved and stopped. Whit judged the direction and the distance. Not so far. Not far at all. Okay, he told himself, the jig is up.

He took one last deep breath and let it go then bulled forwards through the underbrush. He made enough noise to flush all bobcats for miles and he knew it, so he kept the revolver straight in front of him as he ran, thumb on the hammer, ready to plug any moving thing.

He charged through the dense scrub to the first few trees. It was there, right there. He stopped to breathe on the very spot where he knew he had heard the sound. He checked the ground for tracks or a path through the leaves and needles, but it was too dark to tell. If it was a bobcat, it could have gone up the tree. He looked up the nearest ones into the low branches. He waited. No cat moved up there, nothing. A few stars twinkled calmly between the boughs.

He was getting dizzy so he looked down. He had to admit he was feeling none too hot. The ticker wasn't bad, but it wasn't twenty years old any more either.

He stood for almost a minute, wavering slightly. Normality began to return to his chest, but nothing moved again in the woods. Probably a big skunk or coon, he decided, burrowed in somewhere. Oh well, great white hunters get skunked sometimes. It goes with the territory. What the hell. It even crossed his mind that it could be Jolie. He never had seen her. Maybe he would, if he could stand as still as a tree.

Ellie was drifting back towards sleep. Impressions were floating just above her, reshuffling, settling down.

Dana was there. More precisely, Dana's smile. But something was behind it. A shadow. Sadness.

Things were moving over Dana's face quickly, fleeing, fluttering like birds. Shadows darted across her eyes, tiny shadows like bats made on water. Dana smiled despite these things. So sweet, Ellie thought. So sad.

Whit's smile. His sad, funny smile. Standing with his back against the wall. His sports jacket open, the lemon jacket. Standing against the coral-coloured wall, dragging on a cigarette, smiling at her.

It was the wall of the restaurant, the little Cuban place above the harbour. Miami, the second honeymoon. Their other lifetime.

They would never go back there, Ellie had the feeling, every time they talked about it. Maybe that was why she dreamed that image so much. She went back whenever she wanted. Whit was wearing the lemon sports jacket and the funny smile. He stood there until she didn't see him any more.

It was a shame, Whit was thinking. He had looked forward to getting off a few shots. He remembered a pine cone he had seen in one of the trees. Should he? Why not? There was nothing out there. No Jolie anyway. It would be a test of skill at that distance. Would it wake Ellie up? He was far enough away – what did it matter? He was squinting up into the branches, trying to locate the pine cone when it hit him.

He was blindsided, hard. He travelled three feet sideways, into the trunk of a Douglas fir. Something snapped in his chest. The pistol flew out of his hand and out of sight into the bushes. His breath was gone, but he clutched the tree with both hands and stayed upright.

He glanced in the direction of the attack and there was a shadowy form, and eyes – fiery eyes. Sulphurous. He couldn't stop himself – he was thinking, cheap effect.

Then there was blood. He swung his right arm at it and missed entirely, leaving himself open. The first cut

159

was right to left, just above the collarbone. It wasn't the kind of slice a knife might make – it was more of a gash.

Whit actually heard it before he felt it, and when he felt it, it was like no pain he could remember. He went to his knees on a root and listed sideways, and as he did, he fell into the next strike.

It ripped upwards on him, through the eyes. It felt hard and stiff as steel, like a hoe or a garden claw, and as it tore him he tried to scream, but there was no breath. A small blubbering cry choked out as he hit the ground. Then his stomach was heaving and his throat was full and there was no breath at all. Next there was a kind of hollowness – cold emptiness in his brain – and it came like a blessing. He saw and felt nothing of the strikes that followed, the slashes that laid his throat open like a torn paper doll.

When it ended, there was only the sound of hissing, slavering breath among the trees. Soon Whit's attacker stood up. The shadow had a human shape. It stepped back.

Two others, a man and a woman, emerged from the bushes and joined it, steadying it on either side. They led it back into the woods, over the path they had come, away from the road and lights.

They only stopped when they reached a clearing where there was a scant light from the stars and the moon as it passed between occasional clouds. The woman used a handkerchief to clear the attacker's face of blood.

"Just as I told you," Kenji Sukaro said, "she had the strength when she needed it. You know what it feels like. You're different when the call comes."

Kizmet glanced at him. She wiped blood and something black from around her friend's mouth and away from the Japanese girl's beautiful eyes. Kizmet had always envied Nikko's eyes.

"Her next time will be easier," Kenji said. "Come on."

When they wrapped their arms around her small back again, Nikko felt lighter, even frail. They guided her down the hill gently through the woods above Kenji's house.

160

22

On Sunday, two days after Whit's death, Dana and Louis sat with Ellie in the living room of the Norwood home. At least for the moment, they had all run out of things to say. Louis was looking down into the rug, a pattern of nested hexagons, and he counted them going in, then out.

He forced himself to look up at Ellie in the recliner, across from them on the sofa. She didn't look good. In fact, she looked very much the way Louis and Dana expected before they came. Her hair was down, and the blonde had turned a careless washed colour. Grey cheeks, face slack from the pills.

Louis wondered if they should go. Maybe she was tired of people coming by. But leaving her alone wouldn't be good. He was sure she must have considered suicide. He wondered if she was thinking about it even as they sat there. What more could he say to her? Fortunately, Dana broke the silence.

"Do you want somebody to stay with you for a day or two?"

"No, dear. A lot of folks have dropped in and they've been so nice, like you."

The evidence was there, in the bouquets on the tables in the living room and hall. Dana thought flowers would be grizzly before the funeral. Instead she brought a pasta salad which would last for a few days. She and Louis had always liked it, but she had made do with substitute noodles – the real rigatoni didn't exist in Lapis. Besides the flowers, the house had a severely tidied look. Carol Hansen and Mildred Speck were just being helpful, but the pristine arrangement of furnishings and the tightly drawn curtains had made the place into a mortuary.

"My brother and his wife are coming in from Dallas this evening," Ellie continued. "I'll be going back down with them after the service tomorrow. I'll just stay there a little while. Then I'll come back. Maybe sell this house and take a smaller place. I don't think Whit ever liked it that much." Her chin started to tremble.

"Oh, I think he did, Ellie," Dana said quietly. "I'm sure he did."

Ellie just looked at Dana blankly, like a child wanting to believe but not knowing exactly how. Dana tried to think of something positive to say, but she was still thinking when they heard a sound outside the driveway.

"Who is it?" Ellie said weakly, starting to sit up in the recliner.

"You stay there," Louis said. He got up and went to the front window and held the curtain back. "It looks like Lloyd Burris."

He dropped the curtain and headed for the door. Dana could tell something was up.

"What's wrong?" she said.

"Nothing," he said in the opposite direction. "He's got – something on his car."

Louis was out the front door and Dana steadied Ellie as they began to follow. Lloyd and another man were climbing down from the four-wheel-drive Scout as Dana reached the door. There was something on the hood, something like a big grey dog, its head hanging over the side.

Lloyd raised his hand, striding up the gravel drive in his hiking boots. He was in his khaki uniform and badge and he carried a ranger-style hat. A black pistol butt rode in his holster.

"How're you, Louis?" he said. "This is Deputy Rice."

Dana saw Louis shaking hands with the sheriff and the other man, and she tried not to hurry Ellie down the front steps, but she did want to hear.

"Up by Kelsey Lake last night," the sheriff was saying

162

as Dana and Ellie joined them. "It's the one, I'm sure of it. Miz Ferrin, Miz Norwood."

"What – " Dana began.

"A wolf," Louis answered. "The sheriff said it was a rogue wolf – "

"That's right, ma'am." Lloyd Burris was talking to Ellie. "This is the animal that attacked Whit. It's a rogue timber wolf, we think probably rabid." They all began walking to the Scout. "We'll know for sure when we send the head to the lab in Carson City."

They stood looking at it from a few feet away, out of range of the flies. It was a large wolf, and it lay tied across the short hood. The engine ticked beneath it as it cooled. To Dana it looked like a husky, but she could see the difference in its long legs and the mass of its shoulders and the chest under the grey fur.

Two spots, one on the chest and one on the neck, darkened the fur, matting areas the size of a man's hand with blood. There was blood around its mouth too, crusted on the black lips pulled tightly back, and on the exposed fangs. The long swollen tongue lolled out and hung down against the fender.

Dana studied its eye. She couldn't tell for sure what colour it might have been, brown or black or even the husky's ice-blue, but the lifeless eye was a lead-coloured disc. It reminded her for a moment of a button on a grey and red dress she had always liked to wear. Had the wolf stalked a man with that eye? she wondered. Did those fangs do to Whit everything they say had happened?

"Are you sure?" Dana asked suddenly.

The sheriff just looked at her for a moment. Deputy Rice was watching her too from behind dark glasses.

"Yes, ma'am," Burris answered. "The County Coroner came up yesterday for the investigation. He's seen wolf attack. They're rare up here but not unknown. We are in the high Sierras, you know." Then he turned to Ellie.

"We'll be going now, Miz Norwood. If there's anything you need, please give us a call."

"Thank you, Lloyd," Ellie said, staring at the head of

163

the animal, tried and executed by Lloyd Burris for the murder of her husband.

The sheriff and his deputy climbed back into the cab, and through the open door Louis noticed the two rifle bags on the back seat. The Scout backed slowly down the drive, and Dana and Louis guided Ellie into the house. She said she wanted to rest and Dana offered to stay but she assured them she would be fine.

When they reached the car and Louis bent over to unlock Dana's door, two fat black flies were walking along the base of the window. They buzzed up together and he waved them off.

They didn't say anything at first, just exchanged glances as he turned the key. Dana remembered what the sheriff had said. *We are in the high Sierras.* She thought of how magical and carefree it had seemed such a short time before.

23

As Ellie's brother Stewart and his wife Dorinda were pulling into the driveway in the Sedan de Ville they had rented at the airport, Kizmet was on the long leather sofa in Kenji's living room, curling her hair around one finger. Kenji was reading the account of Whit's death in the Sunday paper. He was almost through.

"'An investigation involving the office of the County Coroner and other law enforcement personnel was concluded on Saturday, under the supervision of Lapis Sheriff, Lloyd R. Burris. The funeral for Whit Norwood will be held on Monday, July 22, at 11 A.M. at the Tallac Memorial Chapel.'" He looked up at her over the top of the paper. "We'll go," he stated.

"Sure, I'd want to go anyway," she said.

What Kizmet meant was that even if they didn't have to go for appearances' sake, she would still want to go to Whit's funeral. She had always liked him. He wasn't boring. And his zaniness had just meant that he had real feelings. She could tell.

She was sorry that it had to have been Whit. She would not be telling Kenji that or the old man. It was like anything – if you like what you've got, you play along.

Somebody was laughing behind her on the landing. She didn't have to look – she knew Nikko's laugh a mile away. Kizmet didn't resent it. Nikko had no idea what they were talking about. It was just bad timing. Even though she had done it, she didn't remember what it was really like. Just as well. That was the way it worked, like the brain just shut down.

"And so he goes, 'I have a right to my opinion, don't I?'" The voice was getting closer. They were coming down the stairs.

"Well, opinions are like assholes, you know. Everybody's got one."

Kizmet turned around to watch Lloyd Burris crossing the living room arm in arm with her friend. He had that lazy grin on his face and he was carrying a board-game box. She often wondered how Nikko could be with him; he was so American Boy. Still, he liked her a lot, or he wanted her, at least. You had to want something or somebody very badly to get into this.

"What's up?" Nikko said and passed a joint to Kizmet. She was wearing black tights and the floppy tan pullover with the cowl neck. Kizmet thought she looked okay, a little buzzed but okay.

"You guys are coming too, right?" Kenji said, getting up, heading for a drink. "Eleven tomorrow, Tallac Memorial. We should go in separate cars."

He sounded nervous. He didn't have to be, Kizmet thought, but that was the way he was.

"Right," Lloyd said, and dropped the Scruples box on the table.

"It wouldn't look good," Kenji said, "if any of Whit's friends didn't show."

He dropped ice cubes into a glass and everybody could hear them. Then they all stayed quiet.

165

Kizmet found herself wishing Whit was there, mainly because he wasn't boring. He always had something to say when nobody else could think of anything. The joint had a little fire left. She took a small hit and held it down.

Worry car.

Not so far. Not so close and not so far,

The Cadillac sat in the Norwoods' drive under its own coat of wavering heat. Too far away to see her. They couldn't see her, even if they were sitting in the big brown car. Too far. Not so far but too far.

A lot of them had been there the day before. Walking around in the bushes and the grass, looking down, everywhere inside the big square made by the yellow tape. It was like hunting. Like Easter eggs.

Jolie walked squatting down, peeping just around the bushes. She could be quiet, quieter than birds. But the others were gone now, all gone. They wouldn't see her. Not even if they hid in the big brown car or spied from between the curtains in the house.

She went back a little to the first tree. Then as she was heading towards the big tree, she could feel it. She hadn't seen the body, but she knew it had been there. She knew the way the flies did, or how worms did when they came up from way under the ground.

She edged closer. The toes of her sneakers tested the ground like Geiger counters. She was almost to the tree. She couldn't go any farther. You shouldn't stand there – bad things could happen. Jolie thought of the body in the clearing. It was a place you could never stand again, even after the birds and the white worms and the bugs had emptied it out and the bones had turned to dirt. Not even after the snow went down.

She couldn't stand in the spot by the tree, so she walked steadily, purposefully away. She touched another tree with the palm of her hand and angled towards some low bushes. Dark ferns sprouted there too, and in a patch of sun, some star jasmine with a profusion of sweet-smelling white blooms.

Jolie lay down by the fern. She lay flat on her back and spread out her arms like a dead person. She closed her eyes and lay very still. The little flowers were good to smell. She opened her eyes again, pulled down a branch and sniffed, then let it pop back up. Her eyes followed the line of the branch to the right, down the tiny trunk. Where it met the ground, a bit to the side under a fern, there was something black.

She just looked at it at first. Then she rolled on her side and looked. Get closer. Jolie began to creep in under the spreading fronds of the fern.

Touch first, just with the finger, arm stretched out all the way. Cool. Cool black metal down under the fern. Hot car, wavy hot, out in the drive.

The whole hand next time. Get it. Drag it slow. Heavy. Heavier than sticks and colder. Drag it through the leaves.

She backed out from under the fern and picked it up with both hands. She had never touched one before, but she knew what it was. Her uncle had one. It was way up on the shelf, but she had seen him shoot in the place with the fence. At home, he had rubbed it with a white rag. She practised holding it by the handle. She could keep it safe. She had places.

She stood up and looked all around. Except for blackbirds, no one had seen her. She let Whit's revolver hang straight down beside her leg. She liked the heavy, important feeling. Then she turned and went back the way she had come. There was the hole in the bottom of the tree and the rocky shelf. There was the thorn bush. She thought of several more good places for it and tried to decide on one.

24

"Do you believe it?" Dana was like a caged cat in the living room. Louis sat in one of the old deep chairs and watched her pacing between the sofa and the fireplace.

"Sure, why not?"

"God! It's obvious!" she shot back, throwing her hands out like the hot-headed Italian he used to kid her about being in the early days. Over the years, they had both grown less amused.

"What," he said coolly, "is obvious?"

"That wolves don't go around doing what the newspaper and Ellie's friend – that Mildred – said happened to him. They attack in packs, not alone. That's how they kill animals larger than themselves, not alone."

"Since when have you been an expert on wolves?"

She glared at him. He could see that her fuses were cooking.

"It is fucking common knowledge and you know it."

"No," he said, pausing patronisingly, "I don't. Necessarily. What I do know is that Mildred's version of what happened is probably about as level-headed as a story in *National Enquirer*."

"So do you remember what it said in the paper? 'Horribly mangled. The victim of a violent attack.' Is it all lies, Louis? Is that what you think? Is everybody a liar to you?" Dana was shaking.

"Newspapers are show business."

Her hands were clenched and rage flashed in her eyes.

"You're not listening, goddamn it! Why aren't you?" She just glared at him. "There's a reason you aren't listening, isn't there? What is it?"

"I'm listening," he said, backing off. "I'm listening." He was flashing on Taggart, but there was no way he was going to talk about it.

Dana looked as though she was trying to calm down, or at least be civil. She walked in front of the sofa but didn't sit.

"I want to leave," she said.

"Dana, Whit's death was a shame. But people do die, in all kinds of ways. It doesn't mean – "

"He didn't just die. There's something bad here. Something . . ." Her face started to tremble. "I don't want to be here any more."

She hadn't looked well for several days, but he had tried to

168

ignore it. She was highly strung and she had spells. He had seen it before. In the next instant she burst into tears.

"I want to go home," she cried and sank into the sofa, face in her hands.

"Okay, okay," Louis said. He crossed over and sat beside her and put his arm around her. She leaned against him and sobbed. He tried to think fast. He had to keep the time he needed.

"All right," he said, "we can go back. How about tomorrow afternoon? We can get up and do the beach once more then come back, sauna, and take off. How's that for a plan?"

She looked up at him, less frantic, but with tears still coming. He knew what she was thinking. She wanted to leave that night.

"That way we can take our time," he said. "We'll still have two full days in the city before we go back to work."

Dana thought it over a moment then nodded quietly.

"Okay?" he asked.

"Okay," she said, smiling, but only for a moment.

He felt better. It could still work. He still had time.

Soon Dana was talking about packing and planning the dinner in advance. She wanted to make a potpourri of their perishables, which meant a big salad, creamed herring, cold cuts and cheese. It was a little before five, but she wanted to start on the salad right away so she would have some packing time before dinner.

There was only one Molson's beer left in the refrigerator, and Louis saw his chance. He insisted that they have a good wine for the last supper at Alpenhurst. A jug from the Lapis market wouldn't do. He wanted quality, estate bottled from Napa or Sonoma. He had spotted a good wine shop in Tahoe Vista. Dana protested, but he swore the round trip would take less than an hour.

By the time she agreed, he was wondering how long the real trip would take. He had no way of knowing yet. Later he could say the shop had been closed and he had to pick up something in Lapis.

He left her in the kitchen slicing green peppers, back

169

to the door. He crossed the living room to the stairs, but instead of going up for his keys, he slipped into the den. Then he pushed the door closed carefully, but not so far that the latch would click. He started to take out his wallet for the number but discovered that he remembered it. He went to the phone in the corner.

What did it mean to be doing this? He had been wrestling with the same question for two days. There might not be much to it at all. "Open yourself," the man had said. Wasn't that wise advice? Didn't religion teach that, and psychology? It might be pure hokum, but how would he know if he didn't take the chance? Maybe that's all opportunity really amounted to. Standing open. Maybe his break would only come once. Was fear going to lock him up?

But could Dana be right? Was there something she couldn't quite say going on here? She really did seem afraid, and Louis hated that. He needed for her to feel safe, probably more than she did. He thought of a house and his job and money, and Dana was in those thoughts too. How would he know if he didn't take the chance? The answer was that he would never know. And how could he live with that?

He picked up the phone and pressed the buttons. When the voice answered, Louis surprised himself. He thought he was ready, but perhaps it was something in the tone that caused him to stand speechless, with the receiver carrying Taggart's voice so intimately into his ear. He listened to the old man waiting for a response, and then Taggart broke the silence with a word.

"Louis," he said. It wasn't a question, but a statement, direct and clear. Yes, he went on when Louis could speak to him, he had been waiting. Yes, he would be there.

When Louis arrived at Dunn's Crest the second time, he didn't have to knock and wait. The door was opening as he came up the path.

"It's good to see you again," Taggart said from just inside the door. Louis was surprised at his simple attire: grey pants and loose black shirt like a painter's smock.

170

"I would like to congratulate you," he said as they entered the hall. "You made the right decision." He closed the door and led the way into a room, a different one from their last meeting.

It felt very different. Louis sensed the emptiness most. A few dark oils, heavily varnished landscapes, drawn curtains. A single straight-backed chair sat in a corner of the room and, beside it, an end table. Taggart crossed to the chair and sat down.

"It's the best thing," he said quietly, "for everyone." Louis paused before responding.

"Why are you here?" he asked.

"Because there are those who need me."

"But why here?"

"One must have access to people, don't you agree?" Taggart smiled briefly. "We can theorise in solitude, prepare ourselves and gather our resources. But for our actions to be meaningful, they must be shared by others. The effects of what we do must be known and felt by others.

"We are, as the poet said, destined to play our parts upon a stage. Players come here – and to places like this – seduced by the anticipation of pleasure and by the natural beauties. This place is opportune. And opportunity is the theme of our play, is it not?"

"What kind of opportunity?"

"The kind to match one's needs, one's desires. To order, you might say. Some want, quite simply, wealth. Some, position and influence. Others merely want others very much like themselves."

Louis broke away and crossed the room to one of the paintings. A peaceful stream meandered down a soft summer hill, but he could feel Taggart's gaze on his back. He turned.

"How can anyone promise any of that?"

"You have met certain parties here – beneficiaries of fortune. Seeing is believing, Louis, is it not?"

"But who are you to promise it?"

Taggart only looked at him. Louis felt a silence, deep from behind the old mask, from inside, behind the eyes that

171

seemed old as stones made in the cold ages of the earth. It was as though the eyes held pictures from beyond anyone's remembering – days of ponderous dark clouds and ice on stone, desert days that howled with pestilential winds. The pictures in the eyes interlocked, like inscrutable scratchings on an icon, markings that called up dread in manlike things long before there was a word for Lord.

Finally Taggart glanced at the table beside his chair, and Louis felt snapped awake. He realised that he had seen the small wooden box which rested there without really noticing it. Taggart slid it to the front of the table. The box was teak, Louis guessed, less than a foot long and narrow, the top inlaid with a light wood panel of closer grain.

"I assure you," Taggart said as he looked up, "your trial will not be a difficult one."

Louis looked from the box to Taggart. The word *trial* chilled him. Dana had been right, he realised deep down. Taggart was rotting, miasmal. If you got closer, the rot would spread. But he could be resisted, the old fart. Louis saw himself turning, stepping calmly from the room, opening the front door. There was nothing so all-powerful about him. He was not the blackness. No such thing. No God, no blackness. Must be resisted. Leave this room. Get out. He had no power you didn't want to give him. Get out! He couldn't take a thing unless you gave it away first. Gave it up. Louis felt something inside slipping. Taggart was like quicksand and Louis was over the edge, sinking.

"Do not fear." The voice was even and quiet, almost soothing. "Your call will unlock strength you never knew you possessed. Superhuman abilities are sealed within us all, like the sudden strength of the mother who lifts the car from her trapped child."

The old man nodded towards the box and waited. A moment passed and Louis stepped forwards and picked it up.

As he did, Taggart rose. Then he was out of the room and in the hall and Louis was following. He was feeling light-headed again, as he did after the Madeira. The door opened and he was passing the tall man in the black shirt who only stood quietly like a sentry at a gate.

He could have been sleep-walking. As his foot touched the first step, he was seeing Taggart again, in after-image. The old face was blackening, but his eyes were bright. Then the vision was replaced by images of beasts – a wolf, a goat, a fly, a bat-headed thing with bony ribs and wings of skin. Louis shot a glance back, and Taggart was still there, an old man in the door of a very old house. He descended the other step.

The evening felt warmer than he remembered. He heard the door close behind him, and then he was carrying the small box, unopened, walking down the drive.

Splitting off at an angle, through the yard and around the side of the house, ran a flagstone path, and when Louis came to it, he followed the stones without knowing why. He had passed the corner of the old house but had not yet come to the end of the path that led to the woods when he heard it.

The sound was guttural and hollow, like something howling in a cave. It brought a sickening taste to his mouth, and he wanted to vomit but couldn't. He bent over, clutching the box, and as he did he felt something shift inside. Louis squatted down and held on and tried to breathe. Shadows rolled from both sides, so thick that he could see only the shale flagstone under him and the drops of his own saliva falling on it. The sound was rolling in his head, and he gulped air through his mouth to dilute it and tried to hold it down.

He stared at the stone slab and at the box in the centre of his vision, and when the shadows began to clear, he saw the damp spots left on the teak by his sweating hands. He looked up slowly. There, in the last grass before the trees, a large dog bounded slowly and halted.

It was heavy in the shoulders, grey with white and black markings on its head and tail. He thought of the wolf, but this was no wolf. It was a dog, at least part German shepherd. It bounded a few steps towards him, as if it wanted to play, then stopped in the grass and waited.

173

He could hear its breathing clearly. He could smell its musky scent and moist fur. He realised it was time to open the box.

The lid hinged back. The weapon inside was as impressively wrought as the material which composed it was crude. The knife was all fashioned, both blade and grip, of stone.

He took it by the handle and let the box fall. It seemed to be falling slowly. It smashed to pieces on the stone. The dog was panting. It turned towards the trees and Louis followed.

Running was effortless. It was so easy to breathe, and the air was charged with moist evening smells. Grass rushed by beneath his feet.

As he jogged in among the trees, he could see the grey dog clearly up ahead. It stopped then bounded on again, and Louis crashed through the bushes after it.

He knew he could kill the dog. He felt so strong. He sensed the strength rippling along his arms and in his chest and legs. He squeezed the stone grip as he ran, and it felt like an extension of his hand. Branches clutched at his legs but he hardly felt them. His breathing was smooth.

He dodged the trees, keeping the dog in sight in the twilight. But it was innocent, wasn't it? he thought suddenly. He nearly stumbled. It was an animal, a beast, and it was essentially innocent and neutral. No! The dog knew the same blood hunger he was feeling. In its race memory it heard the same low music of pursuit that Louis heard now, the thundering of hearts and the howling in his ears and the brief, painful cries. It wasn't innocent at all. When he picked up his stride again, he had lost sight of his prey.

He ran on in the same direction and, as he vaulted a log, he spotted the animal again. It had stopped, panting, and was facing him. It seemed only to be waiting.

A short clear stretch lay between Louis and the dog, and he felt like laughing. The knife would sink in at the base of its throat like a deep claw. He could lock its head back and rip down. No pain the animal could give would matter. He felt invincible and terribly free. He charged at the animal as it stood waiting.

174

The steps flew. Louis sucked a breath and leaped.

As his feet left the ground, the dog did also — straight into the air in front of its attacker and, as his knife lashed out into emptiness, Louis saw, only for an instant, a vision that knifed through his own chest like a cold blade.

The dog leaped six feet straight up on its hind legs, but in a horrid mutation, its forelegs and head, ill-formed, contorted and patched with fur, became the arms and head of Noah Taggart.

Then, in the instant when Louis expected hard ground, there was free fall. The hurtling drop over the edge of the stone quarry occupied only a moment of his life, but the moment held them all. The ones at the party. The contest. Before the contest. A set-up. How long before? He and Dana had been chosen. He must get to her, shield her like wings.

Then the flat stone rose to meet him, a great hammer that swung into his shoulders and neck and skull. Louis tried to call out from the stone pit that had been dug to carve headstones, but there was only choking darkness, and Dana on the other side.

The beast of Noah Taggart hovered in the air, surveying the broken body fifty feet below. When it did not move, the dog-beast resettled on the cliff. A snarl came past the fangs, ill-fitting in the human mouth. Another.

Finally it moved away, back through the forest on hind legs, regaining its man-stride. Its thoughts had remained clear, also its sense of irony. To think, it mused, that Louis believed Taggart and the others had wanted him. It stepped out into the grass again and followed the flagstone path around the corner of the house. By the time he passed the white car in the drive and started down the hill, the tall man was walking quickly.

25

The dinner had been ready in the refrigerator for half an hour. Dana was upstairs packing when she heard a noise down below. It could have been a muffled breaking, like a wine glass in a towel.

First she thought she had left something on a ledge and it fell. But the wine glasses she had rinsed and dried were already on the table. Then she imagined that Louis had got back and had a little accident while trying to surprise her. Flowers in a vase? She dropped the jeans into the open suitcase on the bed and went to the door.

"Louis?" she called in the direction of the stairs.

When there was no answer, she walked to the staircase. She listened but heard nothing at all down below, only the slight creaks of her weight on the first stair, and then the second.

"Louis," she called again and stopped.

Four more steps brought her to the landing, and she could see into the living room and part of the den. The first floor was quiet. The white curtains belled a bit in the evening breeze, but that window opened only two inches to its lock. Dana waited a few seconds more then turned back upstairs.

It was depressing. She was tired of starting at her own shadow. She was sick of sleeping badly. But now all that would be ending. She took a deep breath in the upstairs hall and walked back into the bedroom.

Just a minute, she thought. She went into the bathroom, turned on the light, and looked in the mirror. Tired. Definitely. She could do better than that for their last evening. She turned on the cold tap and let it run then bent over and splashed away.

Even as she did, she knew that if there were any other sounds, she wouldn't hear them with the running water in her ears. She had had enough of her own silliness. It was time to grow up. She splashed more water on her face. The goal was to feel as pure as that water again, just as clean.

As she dried off, she decided that after they were back home and settled in for a couple of weeks, they should take a nice short trip, only a weekender, maybe to Santa Cruz or Calistoga. She went back to packing, feeling a little guilty

176

about forcing them to leave early. Still, she knew in her heart that it was the right thing. Nothing could change her feeling about the place. Nothing she could imagine, anyway.

That was what she was thinking when she heard the other sound, the one which she knew instantly was not her imagination, as much as she might have wanted it to be. The creak was familiar, and she knew just where it was. A board in the hall always gave a little when they stepped on a certain spot on the carpet – just to the left of the bedroom door. Her breath caught as she looked up, wanting to see Louis. There was a shadow on the hallway carpet, and then a form in the door. She was almost relieved.

"Hello, Dana."

"What a surprise! How did you – ? I mean, you came in with Louis – "

In the doorway, Brian Thomas just smiled for a long moment. Then he shook his head. He was in his usual casuals – knit shirt and jeans – but nothing else about him looked familiar. His hand rubbed the door frame unconsciously as he stared at her.

"Oh, you got another key, then," she went on, not sure whether she still wanted to be polite. "But where's Rhonda?"

"Back in the city," he said. "Rhonda didn't come for this little visit."

He stepped into the room and Dana took an instinctive step back. He crossed casually to the dresser and fingered one of two porcelain bird figurines on top. Her drawer was standing open, and Dana watched as his hand settled there, somewhere in her clothes.

"The contest, you know?" he said as he looked up. "It wasn't exactly the way it seemed. You see, we wanted you here. More specifically, I wanted you here. The contest was the way of doing that." He forced his hands into his pockets nervously and moved a step closer to the bed. The lines in his face seemed deeper. His eyes looked nearly black.

"It really was the best way to bring you in. You've already met several of the others now. They like you," he smiled

177

quickly. "And for you it won't be so difficult." She started to retreat another step and backed into the night table.

"Don't pull away from me, Dana!" he shouted suddenly. "I've done things for you! I've done things, okay? Okay?" He winced then took a short breath and went on. "It doesn't matter. You were what I wanted and I did things I had to do, and they don't really matter now because you're here. You'll understand later. Believe me, you'll understand."

"Louis is coming back," she blurted. "He'll be back soon, any minute. You back off and we'll just forget this ever happened." Her hand was feeling behind her.

"No," he said simply, "Louis won't be back. Louis will have nothing to say about this. Or about anything."

"I'm afraid," another voice came from the door, "that what Brian says is quite true." Noah Taggart stepped in quietly from the hall.

Dana saw a muscle twitch in Brian's cheek. Her glance shot from him to Taggart.

"No!" she howled. "Louis!" Her hand had found the lamp and she yanked and hurled it.

As Brian feinted, the ceramic base glanced off him and smashed against the wall at the edge of the fireplace. He clutched his shoulder, scowling. Then he stood up and moved his arm in a circle for a moment, testing. His eyes were smouldering and his face was flushed. He broke towards her.

The night table had fallen at Dana's feet, and she kicked it at him, but he hurdled it and hit her with his full weight. She slammed off the headboard on to the mattress and he was on her.

He ripped the buttons on the front of her dress then his wet mouth was on her chest. She tried to get her knee up, but his leg blocked her. The suitcase hit the floor. She thrashed under him and tried to gouge his eyes, but her nails only raked the side of his face. Then he had both her arms, bending them back and up, over her head. He had her pinned to the mattress, arms and legs. Sweat gleamed on his face and the side of his cheek was bleeding. His mouth was inches from hers. Dana clamped

178

her lips shut and whipped her head from side to side, side to side.

Suddenly her arms were free. Brian was sitting up on her thighs, his face blank. Dana saw Taggart behind him, close behind. His gnarled hand was clamping Brian's throat.

In the next moment, Taggart lurched backwards and Brian's body left the bed. It flew the dozen or so feet from the four-poster to the fireplace wall in an instant. She heard the full concussion of his head and shoulders against the stone, but by the time she raised her head, his body had pitched forwards, face-down. His right arm was twitching. Blood was seeping into the oriental rug from the open back of the skull that had cracked like a melon against the stone wall.

Taggart seemed unaffected by the effort as he turned towards Dana. He straightened and watched for a moment, breathing easily. His face softened a bit.

"Brian was a foolish man," he said. "Although his judgement about certain things – about you, in particular – I could admire. You have a quality, something quite rare, which sets you apart from the others. I sensed it the moment I saw you.

"Your life has been a preparation, although you may have denied it to yourself, denied it out of fear. It has prepared you for an important role, invested you with potentials. You do know what I mean, don't you? Though you feel powerless at times, you know that the power is there, deep down, locked inside you."

Dana watched him, unable to move.

"I need your special quality, Dana. Just as you need to become who you truly are. There is much I have to show you. I alone can issue the invitation to your inner one. I can set it free. You will become yourself – splendidly, terrifyingly strong." He extended his arm. His hand hovered in the air before her like a large upturned claw. It moved closer.

Dana screamed and rolled. She toppled over the foot of the bed, her foot catching one of the posts, hitting the floor at a bad angle. On the same floor a few feet away, Brian's face was a mask of blood, wide-eyed, staring into the wet rug. She scrambled forwards on her knees, fell, pulled up her dress and scrambled. Taggart was back there.

As she made the door, she choked some breath in and tried to stand, but she was dizzy and off-balance, and her knee caught the edge of the door frame. Searing pain shot through her lower leg and she screamed and went down again, on hands and knees in the hall. Over her shoulder she saw Taggart in the middle of the room, starting towards her.

Dana crawled like a child on hands and knees, her left knee throbbing with each impact. She reached the stairs and pulled herself up on the newel post. Taggart was in the hall. She blundered forwards, tripping and stumbling down the stairs, but she stayed upright, clinging to the rail.

He would have stopped her then, to keep her from injuring herself further. From where he stood, she looked so pitiful scrambling down. The distance was of no concern to him, the ritual of the pursuit. She would tire and he would be there. She must come closer to him first, if only through exhaustion. The wall inside had started to fall. He could hear her whimpering, battling the front-door lock, frantic with the knob.

Dana flung the door back and ran against the ache in her knee down the front steps and out into the grass. Tallac wasn't far. There could be cars on Tallac.

She only turned when she reached the end of the yard. Taggart was standing, far behind her, in the open door. She had time to take a breath, and another. For the first time, she felt the grass, cool and comforting on her bare feet. Then she turned and limped into the last curve of the drive that led into the trees and to the road.

When she finally did reach Tallac Lane, Dana kept going past the shoulder, turning left, staying in the middle of the pavement. She checked both directions for cars. Running on the asphalt was harder on her knee, and the blacktop, even in the shadows, was still hot from the afternoon.

She made the far shoulder and kept moving. A car would come. She glanced back and there were no cars, but she could see Taggart standing, regarding her coolly from the intersection of the drive.

She slid down the gravel shoulder. Rocks and dirt bit at the side of her leg and knee, but she kept going into the underbrush and trees on the downhill side of the road.

She was putting distance between herself and Taggart, but she couldn't go for ever. She needed a goal and she needed help. She ran to the next tree and doubled over, gasping for breath, trying to think. Could she make it to Lapis through the woods? Was Kenji's house closer?

It was then, as Dana stopped to consider her possibilities, that another pair of eyes spotted her through the trees. The watcher knew who she was. She had seen her at the big house many times. It was because Jolie's hearing was acute that she turned at that moment and spotted the man also, walking quite far above them both on the shoulder of the road. She had seen him before, too, the man with the head of a goat.

As Dana started to run downhill again and the man started after her, Jolie almost cried out, but she clamped both hands over her mouth and crouched low. She stifled the word *Mama* and swallowed it, down deep in her throat.

Dana came to dense shrubs and tore into them. She didn't see the thorns on one, and she was past it before she even felt them. They raked her thigh, and when the pain registered, she fell to her knees and stared down at the tears in her dress and the blood that oozed in lines from her skin. She began to cry. But then she realised. The dense bushes could hide her.

She crawled on her stomach under the shrubs. Her chest hurt from running and she thought that she would vomit soon. She wouldn't be able to go much farther.

Dana worked her way deep into the underbrush. Her stomach was ready to heave, but she kept her mouth shut and ground her teeth. She smelled wet ground. When the bushes ended in a heavy log, she burrowed in beside it, her bare arms and legs in the moss and half-decayed bark and the cool, rotting leaves. She tried to breathe evenly through her nose. She tried to think.

Minutes passed. They were long minutes to her, only to her she knew, but after a while she believed that there had been quite a few of them. Real time had passed with no sign of Taggart. She allowed herself to believe, just a little, that she had eluded him. She would stay there. She could stay until dawn if she had to.

The man was coming. No, no. But he was. He was walking down from the road, straight down. How could he know? But he did. He took slow steps, one after the other. Somehow he was walking straight to her place in the bushes.

Both of Dana's legs were wounded, her left knee throbbing, her right thigh stinging and bloody. She was concentrating on her knee, massaging it, trying to move the leg only inches back and forth quietly. She did not hear Taggart, or sense him, standing like a stern father just on the other side of the fallen log. It was the scream that yanked her to her feet.

It pierced the bushes, chilling and high, a child's terrified cry. It came again quickly, and by the third cry Dana was up. She spotted the source, in the clearing beyond the log, the girl with ratted hair and dirty yellow dress clutching at her mid-section and screaming. Dana wanted to help her, but halfway between her and Jolie stood Noah Taggart.

Dana bolted over the log and started across the clearing in the opposite direction. But the knee had stiffened. It buckled and she pitched forwards and rolled sideways on the ground. Taggart was stepping towards her deliberately, again his black-sleeved arm straight out, his white claw hand forwards.

Dana's leg was a shot of agony, and she nearly lost consciousness. She wasn't even sure of what she saw when Jolie ran in behind Taggart and screamed and he started to turn.

The girl halted and unwrapped her arms from her stomach, uncovering the thing she had been carrying tight against her belly. She heaved it underhand, past Taggart, and it bounced once before coming to rest in the leaves. Dana had only to reach out to grasp the thick black butt of the revolver.

182

She tried to cock the hammer and swing the pistol around at the same time. It went off with a blast that almost stopped her heart, and it kicked up and back but she held on. She didn't see where the shot hit but heard it rip through leaves above her and to the side.

Gun or no gun, Taggart came at her quickly. She steadied the pistol with both hands and centred it on his shirt. She gulped a breath and held it. Then she cocked and fired.

The blast punched a smoking hole in his chest. She saw it. But Taggart was still standing. He was nearly on her. He would fall on her.

She cocked the hammer and squeezed, and another explosion tore the middle of his shirt. A third shot hit just beside the heart. He did not fall. Taggart stood, without faltering, at Dana's feet.

Jolie crouched, wide-eyed. Dana looked up at the old man, standing like a spectre in the choking smoke from the gun. She tried to think of Louis, but it was like trying to scream and making no sound. She could hardly re-create his face. There was no one to save her now. She would not be powerless.

As Taggart bent towards her, Dana cocked the pistol again. Then she pressed the end of the barrel to her temple and squeezed the trigger.

It was in that moment, as the delicate bones on the left side of Dana's skull exploded outwards into fragments, that human blood did finally spatter Noah Taggart, in a bright red fan across his face and black shoulder.

There was a sound in the forest then, an agonised cry, as the howl rose from the old man's gut through his upturned mouth, wrapping itself around the girl's shrieks that followed one another like regular pulses.

From above them, on the road, it might have sounded like howls of wounded animals in the forest. It was the kind of cry one heard only by chance in the wild, where pain came quickly and seldom by accident, long after sundown and far from the house lights of men.

Epilogue

Bougainvillaea. Frieda had always loved bougainvillaea. The blooms, pink and purplish and magenta, always seemed sensual though nearly transparent, diaphanous as summer dresses. Here they grew in profusion in the rear garden, with jasmine and hibiscus, gardenia and hydrangea and oleander.

That was why the veranda overlooking the rear of the property was Frieda's favourite place in late afternoon. She loved the colours of the lush foliage in the spacious walled garden. Behind it, Charlotte Amalie rose into the hills, pastel houses with red roofs crowding the steep slopes. Above the houses was the dark jungle forest.

The brilliant blue of the harbour lay on the other side of the property where the guest houses were, but Frieda preferred the vibrant colours of the garden and the hills. She loved to sit in the white wicker chair on the veranda of the great house, behind her the open windows and the large airy rooms.

"Your tea, missus."

Frieda turned to the tall servant in the starched white shirt and lifted the glass from the tray.

"Thank you, Sonny," she said and he went inside.

She liked Sonny's shirt. It was good to look presentable, even in the off-season. Guests still came through the summer. Hadrian Cove may have gained something of a reputation, but she and Noah wanted it to remain quiet. It suited their purposes much better to cater to those who travelled alone, perhaps even discreetly, anything but anxious for authorities to know their whereabouts. When such persons disappeared, there was seldom any question, never an investigation.

Occasionally – but very rarely – they decided to make a

guest one of their own. Noah had grown more cautious. Frieda had tried to warn him before; his lesson had been a painful one. But, she reminded herself, all that was past now. She sipped the iced tea freshened with mint from the garden.

Was it the bougainvillaea? she wondered. Was that flower the reason she felt a little like a girl again? Or was it being on the island? Or Noah?

She was glad that he had taken the land. It was well-timed for her, she felt, a jungle paradise at her stage of life. In fact, she believed that she had found the place where, her desires having been fulfilled, she could leave a completed life in peace.

The natives were less enchanted with Noah's acquisition, she was aware of that. "The Ghost" some of them called the old European who had purchased Hadrian House and turned the property into a resort. Most kept their distance, but those who worked for Noah were loyal and well-paid – and there were plans for Sonny.

Frieda fanned herself. It was probably Noah, if she had to be honest. He always made her feel girlish in a way she used to despise, childish even. Now she felt so much less at odds with him. Of course, his distraction was gone; that made a difference. He seemed weary, exhausted deep inside, as though he had given up and was waiting for nothing. Still, Frieda believed, it was part of a process and he would change. He would pass beyond it, and she would be there when he did.

Frieda was resting her eyes when she heard shouting from the side of the house.

"Taggart, sir. Taggart, sir!" Casseus was calling frantically, running up the path from the harbour side.

When she saw him, Frieda was afraid. She got up.

"Taggart, sir. Come now. Something terrible. It's St John . . . something. Come now!"

Casseus ran up and halted in front of the veranda, sweat gleaming on the servant's face and soaking his shirt. There was terror in his eyes.

Frieda knew Noah had been resting, but seeing Casseus

186

convinced her that she should wake him. She went to the screen, but she could already see his tall silhouette approaching the door.

"What, Casseus?" Taggart said, stepping out.

"It's St John House, sir. Something there – I can't say. Bad, sir. You come see."

As Taggart headed for the steps, Frieda went with him. He caught her arm.

"Wait here," he said.

"Sonny should come with you."

"I'll go down now," he said calmly. He descended the steps and followed Casseus around the side of the house. Frieda watched him disappear behind the banana trees and went inside to get Sonny.

Taggart passed along under the lush canopy of foliage. He followed the path of coquina slabs that wandered from the house, each step surrounded with clots of foliage, grass and puffs of yellow flowers bright enough to surprise, the colour of butterflies.

Casseus ran ahead, taking the left fork of the path that led to St John's House. It was one of the two-storey stucco bungalows that faced the beach. No one had stayed there for nearly a month.

"There, sir, you see. You see!" Casseus pointed as they neared the house. Then he glanced once at Taggart and turned and ran. He left the path and leaped into the undergrowth, crashing towards the far end of the property, in the direction of the town.

Taggart decided to let him go. The servant was of no importance. The house, however, was different. He could sense something from where he stood.

He moved towards it cautiously. The curtains were drawn, but the windows, as was customary, stood open an inch for ventilation. Taggart leaned forwards to one and put his ear to the opening.

What he heard was not a growl exactly, but a rough, throaty sound, almost a moan. It ended for a moment then began again.

Taggart went to the door and took out his keys. The

187

sound was familiar to him. Recognition brought a trace of a smile to his lips. He inserted the key and stepped inside.

It stood beyond the beds in the corner of the room. The door closed behind him.

From the shadowy form in the corner came the sound. Over and over, one ragged tone, the rough moaning sound meant for the old man.

Even as the one in the dense heart of the shadow came to him in its dance of forms – goat-head, winged one, temple of flies – Taggart was smiling to himself. He had been correct from the first. She had been capable of – important things.

Dana stood taller than Taggart in the corner. Aside from that, she was nearly as he remembered – torn dress clotted with black blood, left side of her exploded skull still open. Her greenish lips were parted slightly and the sound was coming through her teeth. The black eyes burned with a dark fire. She extended her arm to Taggart. Her hand was open.

Noah Taggart breathed evenly. He prepared to let his burden pass. The hand snapped shut.

No one saw it directly. No tourists were strolling the beach at Hadrian Cove in the heat of midsummer. Those who saw in the town of Charlotte Amalie saw only a reflection of the white-hot flash that burst like a magnesium flare, sheeting out over the white sand and the water. The sirens only began when the smoke was spotted at the edge of the beach and then the fire.

By that time, Frieda and Sonny had reached what remained of St John's House: two partial walls around the flames, scattered concrete and smoking debris far out on the sand.

"Lightning, ma'am," Sonny said, steadying Frieda who clung to his arm. "Some terrible lightning or some – "

She knew what Sonny meant. She could feel it too. It was as though her own life had changed hands, and something awful was beginning. Sonny tried to hold her, but Frieda sank through his arms to her knees in the sand.

188

She wanted to be a girl again. She wanted to be running away from there, out across the beach. But as she imagined it, her mind played a trick on her – déjà vu – when the brain slips for a moment and a thought falls straight through into memory. She imagined she had been running on that beach before, but she had been alone and very frightened, and there had been no far trees to run to, and no place to hide.